J.T. EDSON

COLD DECK, HOT LEAD

HarperTorch

An Imprint of HarperCollins*Publishers*

This is a work of fiction. Names, characters, places, and incidents are products of the author's imagination or are used fictitiously and are not to be construed as real. Any resemblance to actual events, locales, organizations, or persons, living or dead, is entirely coincidental.

HARPERTORCH
An Imprint of HarperCollins*Publishers*
10 East 53rd Street
New York, New York 10022-5299

First HarperTorch paperback printing: April 2004

HarperCollins®, HarperTorch™, and ♥ ™ are trademarks of HarperCollins Publishers Inc.

Printed in the United States of America

Visit HarperTorch on the World Wide Web at www.harpercollins.com

10 9 8 7 6 5 4 3 2 1

CARDS TALK . . .
BUT BULLETS TALK LOUDER

"You'll need that deuce of spades to beat me, Bud," Derringer told the younger man, exposing his third jack.

"And I've got it," Bud replied with a grin, flipping over his hold card. "Two t—"

His words chopped off like they had been sliced by a butcher's cleaver. While the required deuce of spades landed face up, it slid off the three of diamonds—that Derringer had added.

A silence that could almost be felt dropped over the room, until Derringer broke it. "That's two all right," he admitted. "Only it makes six cards, which's one too many."

Baffled rage twisted the young man's face. Once more the chair shot from beneath him and his fingers stabbed toward the Colt in its holster.

"You put th—!" Bud began hotly.

His accusation died uncompleted and he froze with his hand not yet touching the gun's butt. Instead of returning the Remington-Thomas cane-gun to behind his chair, Derringer had laid it across his knees in a more accessible position. At the first sign of Bud's move, Derringer caught hold of the claw-and-ball handle, then swung the cane up so that its muzzle lined at Bud's chest.

"It's only my *leg* that's lame, young feller," Derringer warned. "So I'm taking it that you didn't mean what you started to say."

Also by J. T. Edson

Forthcoming
TEXAS KILLERS

For Chris and David Herod
plus "all friends"
at 17 Sapcote Drive

COLD DECK,
HOT LEAD

Chapter 1

THE MOMENT HE PICKED UP THE DECK OF CARDS after changing a hundred-dollar bill for Eli Nabbes, Frank Derringer knew for certain that he was sitting in a crooked game designed to take all his precious winnings and every cent in his pockets.

Fair enough. He had come to Tribune, Kansas, looking for just such a game. Ten days back a young friend had visited the town, become involved in the game, lost all his money and received a bad beating when he complained. When Derringer heard of the incident, he reimbursed his friend's losses and travelled to Tribune with the intention of regaining the money from the gang involved.

Locating the gang took little doing, if a man knew what to look for. While a growing and busy town on the inter-continental railroad, Tribune hardly offered sufficient pickings for two such outfits. Derringer's friend could only give a vague description of the bunch who had fleeced him, due to drink and the beating, but the five players in the game fitted it. So, unfortunately, might any other quintet of casually gathered card players.

Certainly up to that time Derringer had seen nothing to which he could object and set as proof of the others' dishonest intentions. Up to taking the cards only his instincts had led him to assume he might be right.

Knowing the gang would steer clear of him if he appeared in his normal dress as a successful professional gambler, he had made alterations to his clothing. Tall, slimly built, good-looking, his chosen profession prevented his skin from gaining the tan shown by the majority of Western men. So he looked at home in his well-tailored Eastern suit of sober brown, with a gold watch-chain stretching across his vest as an outward and visible sign of wealth. Naturally, wearing that kind of clothing precluded his carrying his normal armament; few dudes owned Western-made gunbelts with an Army Colt in a fast-draw holster. He did not even consider picking up one of the cheap gun-rigs foisted upon dudes by store-keepers in railroad towns, for such would be fatal if the situation arose where he needed his Colt in a hurry. Instead, he placed his reliance on a stoutly constructed twenty-seven-inch-long walking-cane with a claw-and-ball handle, developing a pronounced limp in his left leg to show cause for toting it.

Dressed and equipped suitably, Derringer set off to find the gang. That called for no greater feat of detection than standing in the bar of Tribune's best saloon and complaining in a loud tone at the lack of opportunity for gambling offered by the town. By what seemed like an accident, a well-padded, jovial-faced man spilled Derringer's drink. Insisting on making good for his clumsiness, the man started up a conversation. Exchanging introductions, Derringer learned the other was Lou Ferrely, a store-keeper, and declared himself to be Julius M. Main, salesman and part-owner of a cutler's business.

After which the conversation followed almost traditional lines. Not only did Ferrely know of a card game, straight stud poker for high stakes, but also was on his way to join it. Of course, he did not know how the other players might act if he took along a perfect stranger—— At which point

Derringer angrily demanded to know if the other doubted his honesty. Ferrely hastened to assure him that such a thought never arose and, in proof of good faith, agreed to take him along.

Shortly after leaving the saloon, Derringer witnessed something that made him more sure that Ferrely acted as "steerer" for the gang; picking up victims and taking them to where his companions waited to get to work. Ferrely told Derringer something of the other players in the game. All, it seemed, were reputable citizens but not the kind to mildly accept being put upon. The Keebles brothers, Fenn and Bud, ran a successful ranch, fighting off marauding Indians and outlaws with sufficient regularity to give them considerable proficiency in the use of firearms, but small regard for the sanctity of human life. Operating a better-class hog-ranch, brothel, did not debar Joe Throck from admission to the game—his money spent as well as the next man's when he lost it. However, he had been a top-grade pugilist before taking up his present employment and still kept himself in fighting trim, as anybody who crossed him rapidly discovered. Although Eli Nabbes failed to come up to the other three's standard of toughness, he was brother-in-law to both the town marshal and justice of the peace.

Which, as Derringer knew, served as warning to the victim, should he feel like complaining at a later date, that any kind of objections could be adequately handled. He also recalled that such warnings formed a part of every card gang's armory.

Further evidence came soon after the recital of the gang's prowess ended. A burly deputy marshal halted them and demanded to speak privately to Ferrely. At first Derringer felt concerned, for he recognized the peace officer and wondered if it be mutual. However, he noticed a surreptitious passing of money from Ferrely to the deputy and concluded that it was no more than a pay-off to prevent any warning being given of the game's true nature. The deputy gave Derringer a long look in passing, yet showed no hint of recognition. Nor did Ferrely act as if a warning had been passed, but led Derringer to a small, unassuming saloon in the poorer section of town.

The game was held in the saloon's back room, behind a closed door that prevented the owner or customers seeing what went on. Around the table in the center of the small room sat the rest of the gang—or a bunch of honest citizens gathered for a regular poker game in a place which offered them privacy.

There had only been two vacant seats and Derringer found himself placed with Ferrely to his left, while Eli Nabbes sat at his right. Wearing a black suit, white shirt and neatly knotted tie, Nabbes presented a bird-like appearance. Not an eagle or hawk, but a diminutive red-eyed vireo, or something equally shy and harmless. Beyond Nabbes lounged Joe Throck, big, heavily built, but with thickened ears and a broken nose testifying to his pugilistic prowess. Next to Throck, the middle-sized, unshaven Fenn Keebles wore range clothes, although his hands looked a mite soft and clean for a working rancher. Fenn's place at the far side of the table prevented Derringer from seeing how he was armed. Bud Keebles also wore range clothes of a more dandyish cut, and prominently displayed a white-handled Army Colt in a fast-draw holster on his right thigh.

Everything had been very well done. When Derringer refused to take any more drinks before playing, the others did not press him. Although he watched, and possessed sufficient knowledge to detect most cheating moves, Derringer saw nothing to arouse his suspicions. Nabbes and Fenn played well, showing considerable skill and an appreciation for the finer points of the game. Less skilled, Ferrely displayed noticeable cautious tendencies and only continued when holding good cards. If Ferrely played a tight game, Bud Keebles was loose to the point of foolishness. Time after time the young man stayed in with poor, even hopeless cards, clinging on in the vain hope that a last-minute miracle might save him. Throck's game came somewhere between that of Bud and Ferrely. In fact, they seemed like any other regular gathering of friends playing out their weekly game.

So far Derringer had emerged the winner; although he suspected that at least two pots had been let go to him despite another player holding a superior hand. Everything remained square and above board—until he completed shuffling the deck and placed it for Nabbes to cut. A request for change from the small man, followed by a question from Ferrely, distracted Derringer for a moment.

Nothing seemed changed when Derringer returned his attention to Nabbes and broke down the hundred-dollar bill. Then Nabbes completed the cut and Derringer picked up the cards ready to deal. Instantly he knew the moment had come. A flicker of smug satisfaction crossed Throck's surly features and a mocking, knowing grin played on Bud's lips. Small signs that might have gone unnoticed but for one thing. The deck Derringer held felt different from when he last handled it.

During half an hour's fast action play, the friction raised by shuffling, dealing and handling had made the cards grow warm to the touch. Yet the deck Derringer held felt cooler than when he had manipulated it during the shuffle.

Although he gave no sign of it, Derringer knew what had caused the remarkable change in temperature. While Ferrely had diverted Derringer's attention, Nabbes had exchanged the cards used up to that time for an identical deck specially prepared to encourage heavy betting on the victim's part. Then, despite everything seeming to be in Derringer's favor, he would lose the hand on the call.

Already Derringer's winnings covered the amount the gang had taken from his friend, with enough over to make the trip worthwhile. However, he stood to lose it all, and more, on the hand he was about to deal. Nor could he see any way out at that moment. To fold would arouse the gang's suspicions, as they were sure to create the impression from the start that he held the best hand. It had been his intention to leave the room, under the pretense of going to the back-house, before the cold deck came in, but had left the move too late. So he could only go along and look for a way out.

Calmly, without any hint that he knew of the substitution, Derringer dealt each man his hole card face down. Already an idea had begun to form; not the kind one would select given dealer's choice in the game, but better than nothing under the circumstances. Thinking over the idea, Derringer flipped the players the first of their up-cards.

On completion of the round, Derringer found he had the jack of hearts showing and jack of spades in the hole. Then he studied what his opponents held. Ferrely showed the queen of spades; Bud Keebles, the four of spades; Fenn, the eight of spades; Throck, the nine of hearts and Nabbes the five of hearts. Unless Ferrely had a second queen in the hole, Derringer's pair of jacks made the best cards on the table.

"Queen to bet," Derringer stated.

With none of his earlier hesitation, Ferrely opened the pot for ten dollars. Bud promptly raised it to thirty, despite the apparent weakness of his hand. However, he had done the same thing before, so the move might have passed unnoticed if Derringer did not already suspect skull-duggery. When Fenn stayed, Derringer knew for sure the deal was rigged. A man of the "rancher's" ability did not stay in as third man even if he held a second eight in the hole. Staying on the nine might have proved nothing the way Throck played, but he also raised and Nabbes remained in the game.

With the betting completed, Derringer flicked
out the second of the up-cards. Ferrely caught the
ace of spades, giving him the makings of a good
hand. It seemed that Bud was following his normal
loose style of play by sticking in with no more than
the six of spades falling his way. Nor did Fenn
seem to strengthen his hand by receiving the king
of clubs. An eight of clubs to Throck, followed by
the ten of hearts to Nabbes and then Derringer
dropped the jack of clubs to himself.

"I always say if you've got 'em, you might's well
use 'em," Derringer commented with a winner's
grin. "She's loose for fifty simoleons, gents."

"I ain't scared," Ferrely declared, but did no
more than cover the bet.

However, Bud once more raised and the betting
round saw the pot swell in a manner likely to cause
an unsuspecting lucky player to be reckless. None
of the other players dropped out and with the wa-
gering completed Derringer dealt again.

"King of spades for a royal straight, Lou," Derringer announced as he dealt. "Three of spades for
you, Bud. Ace of hearts for Fenn. Seven of spades
to help Joe's straight, another five for Eli and the
little nine of clubs for me. Looks like you boys
aren't trying to beat me. Anyways, I'll open for
fifty again."

"Your fifty and the same again, seeing's how a royal flush licks two jacks," grinned Ferrely.

Raise and re-raise followed, during which Derringer studied the other hands to estimate where the danger lay. By the time he had completed the fourth and final round of up-cards, he knew that only one hand could possibly beat him.

Although his last card had given Ferrely the ace, king, queen and ten of spades showing, he could not hold a royal straight flush when the required jack of the suit lay in Derringer's hole. So, even if he caught the jack of diamonds for a straight, or a spade to give an ordinary flush, the nine of spades which fell to Derringer made a full house that beat either.

Fenn Keebles received the ace of diamonds as his last card and at best held only three of a kind. A ten of hearts left Throck with a four cards straight open at each hand; fair strength, but woefully inadequate in the face of a full house.

Like Derringer, Nabbes finished showing two pairs; but his highest were only tens and matching one of them did not beat three jacks backed by two nines.

That left Bud, and Derringer knew the danger must come from him. Such a hand would never be dealt with the mere intention of increasing the victim's eagerness. Bud's exposed hand consisted of the three, four, five, six of spades. Given the deuce of that suit in the hole—which Derringer felt sure it was—that made a straight flush and licked the pants off any full house.

Give them their due, Derringer mused, the gang knew how to rig a deck of cards and the best ways to wring every advantage from doing so.

At no time had there been a hand exposed on the table with sufficient power to drive out a cautious player. Receiving the jack of spades in the hole prevented the victim from fearing Ferrely might hold a royal flush. An unsuspecting player would probably be gloating over the fact that he could allow Ferrely to make a bluff of holding the top hand. Throughout the game Bud had exhibited a reckless disregard for the rules of sensible betting; so his sticking in on such apparently unpromising cards should arouse no suspicion. As the odds against being dealt a straight flush in the first five cards stood at 72,193.33 to one, a player might be excused in overlooking the possibility of Bud catching such a prime hand. More so when twelve cards of the spade suit could be accounted for and the seven, being exposed in Throck's hand, left the possible straight open at one end only.

After the discovery that Bud did indeed hold the

straight flush, Derringer would have small chance of making a complaint stick. It could be pointed out that he had shuffled and dealt the hand, although there would be no mention of the fact that the deck he used was not the one played with up to that point in the game.

Having kept a careful watch, Derringer knew that Bud had failed to take more than a quick peek at the corner of the hole card. So the plan the gambler had thought out stood a chance of succeeding. However, he needed a diversion of his own if he hoped to be able to put it into operation.

"Come on, Julius," Ferrely said, before Derringer found time to place the remainder of the deck in the center of the table. "It's you to open."

Clearly Bud was just as eager to commence the slaughter, for he added his voice to Ferrely's in a request for immediate action. Derringer saw an annoyed frown come to Nabbes' face and the little man threw a warning glare at the youngster. It seemed that Fenn and Throck also felt Bud was making things a mite too obvious, for they directed scowls in his direction. Seeing his chance, Derringer took it.

On being invited to sit in at the game, Derringer had rested the walking-cane on the back of his chair. Considering the time to be right, he nudged the cane in what appeared to be an accidental manner. Falling, the claw-and-ball handle struck the floor hard enough to make the cane show in no uncertain fashion that it possessed another purpose than supporting a leg "injured in the second battle of Ball Run." The crack of a shot sounded, flame spurted from the ferrule, the cane bounced in uncontrolled recoil and a bullet drove into the rear wall of the room.

At which point Derringer received all the diversion he could hope for. Trying to throw back his chair, rise and draw his gun all at once, Bud Keebles tripped. He collided with his brother as Fenn also tried to rise with right hand fanning across to the Colt bolstered at his left side. Springing up, Throck twisted around to see where the bullet had struck. Although Ferrely left his chair with a bound, dropping his gaze to the smoking ferrule of the cane, Nabbes did not move. Instead the small man whisked a Remington Double Derringer from under his jacket, but could not prevent his eyes turning down to study the cause of the confusion.

With all the others looking at either the lead-punctured wall, or under the table to see what caused the shot, Derringer found himself unobserved. Like a flash he slid the top pasteboard from the deck, reached across and placed it carefully upon Bud's hole card. So quickly did he move that he completed the addition to the other hand and started to make his apologies before the rest of the players could turn their eyes in his direction. Nor did the extra card show, being placed squarely on top of the vital deuce of spades that gave Bud the only hand to beat Derringer's full house. Everything now depended on the gang's reaction when they discovered that their cold deck had somehow gone wrong.

Chapter 2

"I'm sorry, gents," Derringer apologized, placing the depleted deck on the table and bending to retrieve the still-smoking cane. "That was damned clumsy of me, but I've never known it to be so light on the tri——"

Before Derringer could finish, or any of the gang do more than look around the table, the connecting door flew open and the men from the bar-room entered.

"Damn it, Nabbes, I said no shoo——!" began the owner, then his words trailed off as he saw Derringer seated at the table and clearly not injured in any way.

"It was an accident, barkeep," Derringer announced. "I knocked my cane-gun on to the floor and it fired. Damned if I knew it had such a light trigger. Anyways, nobody's hurt."

Apparently the explanation satisfied the saloon-keeper, for he turned and herded the customers from the room. Derringer then gave his attention to the other players, sensing that his explanation had been at least partially accepted. Yet he felt that he should amplify his reason for possessing such an unconventional walking-cane. His pose as a businessman provided an acceptable excuse.

"I often carry a tidy sum around with me and go places where I might need some protection," he remarked, laying the cane on the table and reaching into the fob pocket of his jacket. "This comes in real useful then, and takes folks by surprise."

"You can say that again," Nabbes breathed, resuming his seat and signalling the others to take their places around the table. Clearly he did not want Derringer thinking about the comment made by the saloon-keeper on entering, for he continued, "What is that thing, anyways?"

"A Remington–Thomas cane-gun," Derringer replied, taking what looked like a cigar-case from his pocket and placing it open on the table. "I'm sorry for being so clumsy, boys. Only this gun's never misfired before. Maybe I'd best send it back to the Remington factory and have them look it over when I get home."

While speaking, he tugged at the claw-and-ball knob, drawing it and the upper section of the casing away from the barrel of the cane. An empty cartridge case flipped out of the open breech as a flat spring-catch snapped up to hold the mechanism in a firing position. Before any of the men could make comment, Derringer took a .38 bullet from the open case and slipped it into the cane's breech. Sliding the handle and casing back to their original position, he returned the cane to its previous harmless appearance.

"You was walking on that cane," Ferrely said, a mite accusingly, showing he understood a basic fault of that type of weapon.

"I can't walk very well without it," Derringer lied, dipping into the open ammunition case again.

"I thought you couldn't shoot one with its ferrule plug in," Nabbes said.

"You can't with most of them," Derringer admitted. "But Josh Thomas came up with the answer for Remington."

With that Derringer showed the others the thing he had taken from the case. It proved to be a piece of cork shaped to plug the barrel-hole of the ferrule. Only the Remington–Thomas cane-gun offered such a satisfactory method of keeping dirt out of the barrel, while still allowing the bullet to be fired immediately. Other such weapons relied upon a wooden tampion which fitted so tightly that it must be removed manually before shooting—failure to do so resulted in at least a burst barrel—or so loosely that it fell out and was lost. Held in place by friction, the cork plug of the Remington–Thomas cane-gun retained its position but could be thrust out of the ferrule by a discharged bullet without risk of damage.

"That's neat," Nabbes commented, after Derringer finished reloading and explaining the cane-gun's virtues. "It's the first I've seen."

"Let's play cards!" Bud growled, eager to lay hands on the pot he knew to be his. However, he too found the gun interesting. So much so that he had not examined his hand and made a premature discovery of the extra card it now held. "It's you to bet, mister."

"Seeing what's just happened, don't you reckon we should call it a dead hand, gents?" Derringer inquired, looking at the others.

"No!"

The word popped out of Bud's mouth like a cork from a champagne bottle and his eyes remained glued on the money already in the pot. Although

Nabbes made a pretense of asking the others, none of them appeared willing to follow Derringer's suggestion that they declare the game null and void.

"I'd say you've a real powerful hand there, Bud," Derringer remarked. "But there're too many spades showing for you to have it. So I'll just start her for a hundred and see how it goes."

Sound strategy and the course an unsuspecting man might easily follow. Certainly none of the gang showed that they regarded Derringer's opening bet with distrust.

"I'll see that and raise the same," Ferrely announced, making the play one might expect when possessing Derringer's knowledge of the jack of spade's whereabouts.

If anything Bud acted too eager and Derringer caught Nabbes flashing the youngster a warning signal. Apparently the slight inclination of the head told Fenn and Throck their course of action, for both folded their hands and quit the pot.

"This's too hot for me too," Nabbes remarked, tossing his cards into the deadwood.* "You boys settle it between you."

"I reckon I'll just see that bet and raise it again," Derringer said.

---

* Deadwood: The remainder of the deck and discarded hands.

Earlier in the game he had contrived to give the impression of being involved in a business deal with the local railroad supervisor and Wells Fargo agent, hinting that both would be remunerated by his company for their part in influencing the two organizations employing them. In any railroad town, an important company official like the supervisor packed a whole heap of weight. So did the Wells Fargo agent. Enough for a friend, or business associate putting money their way, to make good any complaint he might wish to raise. Even if the marshal received a pay-off from the gang, he would not ignore a complaint from such a person.

It seemed that the gang accepted Derringer's story, for they showed no sign of giving him cause to complain. With a less influential victim they might use the technique known as "sandbagging"; re-raising between them until lack of money caused him to fold. Derringer's supposed friendship with Supervisor Deal and Agent Miggers prevented them from making so blatant an attempt on his wealth. Instead, the three men discarded their hands while Ferrely did no more than see the bet. Once more Bud raised, but Derringer could either see the raise or increase on it.

"I reckon I'll just see that," Derringer said.

"You lick me, that's for sure," Ferrely replied, folding his cards.

"You'll need that deuce of spades, Bud," Derringer told the youngster, exposing his third jack.

"And I've got it," Bud replied with a grin, flipping over his hole card. "Two t——"

His words chopped off like they had been sliced by a butcher's cleaver. While the required deuce of spades landed face up, it slid off the three of diamonds added by Derringer. A silence that could almost be felt dropped over the room, until Derringer broke it.

"That's two all right," he admitted as the others stared with bugged-out eyes at the red-spotted addition which had ruined their chances. "Only it makes six cards, which's one too many."

Under the rules of the game, holding an extra card gave Bud a dead hand and caused him to forfeit any hopes he might have of winning the pot. Nor could he blame anybody but himself for the mistake.

Almost a minute ticked by without any comment to Derringer's words, as the discomforted cheats tried to work out where their carefully arranged scheme had gone wrong. Nabbes felt sure that the three of diamonds had not been accidentally stuck on top of the deuce of spades when he arranged the deck that afternoon. Yet he also failed to see how Derringer had managed to make the addition. There had been no time when their proposed victim was not under observation——

Except when the cane-gun fell to the floor, fired and drew everybody's attention from the table.

Yet that would mean "Main" suspected them, or had grabbed the opportunity to make sure his full house could not be beaten. Nabbes wondered which it might be; and how he should deal with the situation.

Reaching the same conclusion as their leader, although somewhat slower than he arrived at it, the rest of the gang waited to see what Nabbes wanted them to do. All but Bud, that is. Baffled rage twisted the young man's face. Once more the chair shot from beneath him and his fingers stabbed toward the Colt in its holster.

"You put th——!" Bud began hotly.

Next moment the young man's accusation died uncompleted and he froze with his hand not yet touching the gun's butt. Instead of returning the cane to behind his chair, Derringer laid it across his knees in a more accessible position. At the first sign of Bud's move, Derringer caught hold of the claw-and-ball handle, then swung the cane so that its muzzle lined at the other's chest. The table was not wide and Bud saw the deadly ferrule so close to him that it could not miss directing the bullet-ejected cork plug into his body.

"It's only my *leg* that's lame, young feller," Derringer warned. "So I'm taking it that you didn't mean what you started to say."

Shock numbed Bud as he realized the perilous nature of his position. No Western court would convict "Main" for defending himself against an accusation of cheating, followed by the invariable attempt to back the words with hot lead, should he shoot.

And from all appearances "Main" knew how to handle the cane-gun with some skill. Not a suspicious point in itself. The War between the States had taught even Eastern dudes skill in the use of weapons and many a travelling salesman had learned to be nearly as tough or deadly as a trained range country gun-fighter.

Nor could Bud see any sign of help from the rest of the gang. Maybe they wanted to cut in, but could see the danger of such an action. "Main" held the cane-gun with his forefinger on the trigger-stud. Any hostile move or attempt to grab the weapon might cause him to press the stud, and at that range he could not miss. So Fenn Keebles, probably most concerned about Bud's welfare, Throck and Ferrely sat still and waited for their leader to give a lead as to their actions. They did not have long to wait.

"Take it easy, Julius," Nabbes said in a placating tone. "Bud spoke out of turn, but it was only because he's disappointed. Who wouldn't be? I don't figure that he meant it."

"The h——!" Bud started with some heat.

"It was your own fault for not checking the hole card before you started betting," interrupted Nabbes, scowling at the youngster. "You can't blame Julius for that."

"Look here," Derringer said, resting the cane on the table but not taking his hand from the handle, "if the young feller feels so bad about it, I'm game to split the pot with him."

A generous offer if the game had been straight; and even under the circumstances it stood to show its maker a good profit. All the gang had bet heavily to keep Derringer in the pot. Apparently the offer relieved the tension, for the other men doubted if a suspicious player would make it.

"Now that's a real sport talking!" enthused Nabbes, while the rest waited for his reactions to the offer. "Only I don't think it's right for us to impose on Julius that ways."

"I go with Eli on that," Fenn went on, before the surprised Bud could comment. "Come on, Bud. Show Julius that us Keebles ain't poor losers."

Interest in upholding the Keebles family's honor

did not prompt Nabbes to make the suggestion. As Derringer hoped, the little man felt uncertain as to how the extra card reached Bud's hand. So Nabbes wanted the affair smoothed over to give them a chance to recoup their losses and show a profit without recourse to violence.

Slowly, reluctantly, Bud sank into his chair. "Go on, take it," he said sullenly. "It's your pot."

"Thanks," Derringer answered, drawing the money toward him and stacking it into a thick pile. "What say you boys let me buy you a drink before the next hand?"

"We can have them sent in," Nabbes remarked.

"Sure," agreed Derringer. "But if we go out to the bar, it'll show those fellers everything's friendly and that the shot was an accident. That way they'll not start spreading lies around."

"Maybe the walk'll change Julius' luck, Eli," Ferrely commented, making Derringer's point stronger.

"In that case I'm all for going out to the bar," Nabbes agreed. Then a frown flickered to his face as he saw that Derringer had placed all the paper money into a wallet. "Aren't you coming back with us, Julius?"

"Sure I am," Derringer replied, dropping the wallet into his jacket's inside pocket, then putting the ammunition case away. "But I thought that the bartender'd be sending somebody in here to clean up while we're at the bar."

"In this place?" scoffed Nabbes. "Why, we had to clear the cigar butts from last Friday night's game off the table when we came in this evening."

"There's nothing for me to worry about, then," grinned Derringer, withdrawing the wallet and tossing it on to the table. "I'll just take the silver along to pay for the drinks."

"Sure," Nabbes agreed. "We may as well have something out of you, hey, boys?"

At the bar, Derringer bought a round of drinks. Then he set about lulling any remaining suspicions. He told a couple of gambling jokes and laughed at one Ferrely countered with. When Bud began to show signs of restlessness, demanding that the game be resumed, Derringer remarked that a trip out back was called for. Hoping for a negative answer, he asked if any of the gang wanted to go along. The hope materialized. In fact, the gang welcomed an opportunity to hold discussion without their victim being present. Thinking about the wallet lying on the table, all felt certain that Derringer would return. So they allowed him to leave unescorted.

Probably all the saloon's customers, and certainly the owner, knew what kind of game Nabbes ran. However, he saw no reason for letting them learn too much about his business. So he stifled unsaid Bud's query about the appearance of the extra card and led the way into the back room. Gathering around the table, the gang each received more playing money from Nabbes' reserve. Nabbes' angry snarl stopped Ferrely opening Derringer's wallet in a premature attempt to regain some of their losses. If the victim found on his return that somebody had tampered with his wallet, he would pull out of the game fast and yell for the law.

The matter of the extra card came in for heated discussion, with recriminations levelled but no solution reached. Then the gang became aware of how much time had elapsed since their victim went out back. Everything was ready, a second cold deck in Nabbes' pocket fixed to trim "Main" to the bone when he returned.

Just as Nabbes decided to send Fenn out back to collect their victim, the door opened. Any relief the little man felt died away when he saw who entered. It was the burly deputy who had stopped Ferrely in the street. Ambling across to the table he grinned at the surprised faces. Receiving payment to ignore the game's existence, he never made an appearance at the saloon's back room when a victim might be present.

"Not playing, boys?" he asked. "Did the mark get wise and pull out?"

"He's gone to the john, is all," Nabbes replied.

"Then it warn't him I saw headed away from here just now? I figured it couldn't be. Feller I saw didn't limp at all."

Knowing that the deputy had not come merely to make casual conversation, Nabbes snatched up the wallet. While looking exactly like the one into which "Main" had stuffed his winnings, the wallet differed in a major respect. Instead of money, it held only sheets of newspaper cut to a suitable size. That meant "Main" knew what kind of game he was bucking and had come prepared with a duplicate wallet. He had made the exchange under the pretense of pocketing his winnings and left a worthless dud so they would raise no objections to his going from the building.

"Where'd you meet him, Lou?" Nabbes gritted, seething with fury but controlling it with an effort.

"At the Golden Spike——"

"He's not there," commented the deputy.

Money changed hands before the peace officer parted with the necessary information. In addition to explaining how he had seen Derringer passing and had trailed him to the Talbot Hotel, the deputy promised not to be around when the gang went calling on him. While the price was high, Nabbes knew a failure to pay it would see the deputy sticking close to their victim and protecting him. However, the deputy threw in a piece of information as a bonus. He told how he had visited the trail-end town of Mulrooney to collect a prisoner and had seen their "victim" wearing a deputy marshal's badge. One name sprang to mind among the deputies who supported the Rio Hondo gun-wizard, Dusty Fog,* as being able to pull off such a trick.

"Frank Derringer!" Ferrely yelped, bristling with indignation as he rounded on the deputy. "Damn it, Barney, you never let on—"

"I didn't recognize him earlier," the peace officer replied blandly. "It was dark, you mind. But he's Frank Derringer sure as you're born."

Due to his work against them in Mulrooney,** crooked gamblers regarded Derringer as a renegade who turned on his own kind, although he never had come into their category. If anything, the discovery of their "victim's" identity increased the gang's determination to take revenge. As soon as the deputy left, Nabbes began arranging how they should get it.

---

* Dusty Fog's story can be read in the author's "Floating Outfit" novels.

** Told in *The Trouble Busters* and *The Making of a Lawman*.

While Nabbes and Ferrely remained at the saloon to establish an alibi, the Keebles brothers and Throck would leave by the back room's window. Warning the trio not to go too far in their revenge, for only the one deputy on the marshal's staff accepted their bribes, the little man watched his companions depart. Then he told Ferrely to fetch in a round of drinks and spread the story that the victim had sent the deputy with news that urgent business had called him away.

Having made their exit through the window, the trio went by the back streets to the Talbot Hotel. Without the deputy's information, they might have spent time searching in the wrong places: the railroad or Wells Fargo depots, livery barns or the fancy Granada Hotel. Certainly the Talbot would have been a later choice, tried when the others failed to produce their man. With luck they ought to take Derringer by surprise. Fenn hoped that they would. Any man who wore a badge under Dusty Fog, even if taken on as a gambling consultant, packed sand to burn and possessed considerable gun-savvy.

In its day the Talbot had rated as Tribune's best hotel but the railroad's arrival had caused a larger, more luxurious establishment to usurp the claim. Now the Talbot drew a less wealthy class of trade,

being unable to compete against the superior at-
tractions of its rival. The type of clientele who now
used the Talbot did not expect that their baggage
be carried to their rooms for them, so the hotel dispensed with the services of its bell-boys. Nor was
the reception desk constantly manned. The night
clerk spent most of his duty hours in the room behind the desk and only emerged when somebody
rang the bell to draw his attention.

Aware of the prevailing conditions, Fenn laid his
plans accordingly.

"We'll see if we can find out which room he's
using from the register," he told the other two.
"Then we'll bust in, pistol-whip him down, grab
the money and light out fast."

"Maybe one of us should oughta watch the
back," Throck remarked. "If he gets wise to us
coming, he might bust out that ways."

"You do that, Joe. Bud and me'll go in after
him."

As that part of the affair offered less risk,
Throck agreed without argument. Even if Derringer broke out, he would not expect to find another enemy waiting. In any case, it would be
better to have Bud where Fenn could exercise
brotherly control over him.

Entering the deserted lobby, Fenn and Bud

crossed to the desk. Clearly Derringer did not expect his disguise to be pierced, for the brothers
found his name to be the last entry in the book.

"Room eighteen, Bud. That's upstairs at the
back. Can't say I like that."

"We could lay for him in the alley," Bud suggested.

"He might not come out until morning and the
boys can't stall at the saloon for that long," Fenn
replied. "We'll just have to chance it. Let's go."

On reaching the door marked "18," the brothers paused for a moment. Fenn hesitated when Bud
gestured toward his gun, then nodded. While not
wanting gun-play, the elder brother realized it
might come if they failed to take Derringer by surprise. If the gambler found himself covered by two
revolvers, he was less likely to resist.

Although the brothers had never been peace officers, they knew what to do. Ducking his shoulder, Fenn charged into the door. It burst open with
a louder crash than he liked, but that could not be
helped. Having gone that far there could be no
turning back. So he lunged forward into the room
with Bud on his heels and his Colt in hand. Both
could see all they needed, for a lamp glowed
brightly on a bedside table.

Instead of being grateful for the illumination to

make their work easier, the brothers suddenly found themselves wishing the room was in darkness. Fenn was the first to realize that their plans had gone wrong. Skidding to a halt, he stared at the bed. His thoughts simply on the chances of finding an excuse to shoot Derringer, Bud swerved around his brother and stopped just as abruptly.

The door clearly carried the number "18," but Derringer did not occupy it. A big, heavily built woman wearing a nightgown and mob-cap sat reading in the bed. Even as the fact registered itself in the brothers' minds, she dropped the book. Jerking the covers up to chin level, she cut loose with a scream loud enough to jolt a dead Indian to his feet. Nor did she content herself with just the one, but let out screech after screech in a growing crescendo.

"Wha——!" Bud croaked, staring at the woman. "Who——?"

Unable to supply an answer to the question, Fenn wasted no time in thinking about the matter. Already he could hear voices raised in the adjacent rooms and knew there must be no delay in departing. Western folks tended to shoot first and ask questions afterward under such circumstances. So Fenn acted with speed.

"Get the hell out of here!" he snapped, thrusting his brother through the door and following him.

Dashing along the passage, the brothers bounded down the stairs and across the reception hall. They ignored the night clerk's yell, leaving the building at top speed and without waiting to debate where they had gone wrong in locating Derringer.

Chapter 3

AFTER LOOKING BACK TO MAKE SURE THAT NONE
of Nabbes' gang was watching him, Frank Derringer entered the saloon's back-house. Sitting on
the box, he removed his left boot. From it rolled
the small stone which had helped him retain his
limp. Despite his comments in the bar-room, he
made no use of the back-house's facilities. Replac-
ing the boot, he stepped from the building. Still nobody was watching. Apparently leaving the
substitute wallet had satisfied Nabbes that their
"victim" meant to return and he suspected nothing. A faint grin came to Derringer's face as he
thought that the gang would have a long wait.
Then he walked off into the darkness.

Not knowing his way around Tribune, Derringer turned alongside the saloon and on to the
street. Then he headed toward the Golden Spike,
where he had met Ferrely and from where he could
find the Talbot Hotel. Once clear of the small saloon Derringer expected no trouble. If the gang
had not accepted his story, one of them would have
accompanied him to the back-house. So he strode
along the sidewalk, taking no special precautions
to keep out of sight.

The burly, bribe-taking deputy saw Derringer
passing a lighted window across the street. Drawing back into an alley, the peace officer watched
the other go by. Then a grin twisted the deputy's
face and he started to follow the gambler, but kept
the street between them and to the rear.

Entering the lobby of the Talbot Hotel, Derringer's glance went to the front desk. The sight of
the register recalled to him that he had given his
correct name on arrival. Then he remembered the
deputy knew him from Mulrooney. Maybe the
man had failed to recognize him as Dusty Fog's
gambling-expert deputy, but Derringer did not believe in taking unnecessary chances.

Having decided on his course of action during
the train journey to Tribune, Derringer had
booked into the Talbot using his own name. Then

if the gang should come hunting for "Julius Main," they might overlook "Frank Derringer" when checking the register. But the fact that the deputy knew him had changed that.

The night clerk had already disappeared into his room as Derringer entered. Crossing to the desk, the gambler studied the open register and found his name second to last in the entries. Looking back over the previous few pages, he found nobody listed as occupying room eighteen. So he picked up the clerk's pen from the ink-pot. By adding a stroke before his room number, he made it appear that he occupied eighteen instead of eight.

Glancing at the key-board, he saw number eighteen's hook was empty. For a moment he hesitated, then decided that even if there should be somebody in occupation the person would be unlikely to come to harm. Unless he misjudged his man, Nabbes would hesitate to create a great disturbance and, as far as possible, avoid gun-play.

So, even if the gang succeeded in locating him and fell for the trick, Derringer doubted if they would enter the room with roaring Colts. Any other way they would discover their mistake in time. Then, most probably, their only thought would be to leave the hotel as soon as possible.

Satisfied that he had covered his tracks, Derringer went to his room and entered. Before lighting the lamp, he gave thought to his escape should the ruse fail. Set at the end of the hotel, room eight offered the advantage of two windows. One of them opened on to the rear of the building, while its mate offered a splendid view of the side alley. Derringer settled on the latter, should the need for a hurried departure arise, for it offered access to front or rear of the hotel.

After raising the side window's sash, he drew both sets of curtains. When sure that nobody could see into the room, he lit the lamp. Locking the door, he thrust the only chair's back under the handle as an added aid to securing the entrance and commenced his preparations to leave Tribune on the midnight train.

By that time the gang would at least be suspicious, or might even have already examined the wallet and know he did not intend to return. In deciding where they might locate him, they would most likely try the more opulent Granada first. So he meant to stay in his room until almost train time, then head for the depot.

With that thought in mind, Derringer stripped off his dude suit. On the bed, ready to be worn, lay his more usual style of clothes. Given just a touch of luck, the gang—looking for the dude-dressed "Main"—would ignore a typical range-country professional gambler. The only thing that might arouse their suspicions would be the Remington-Thomas cane-gun. Not that Derringer intended to leave it behind. If he carried it along the top of his grip, it could go unnoticed.

While making his plans, Derringer changed into the gray trousers, frilly-fronted shirt, string tie and fancy vest. Before donning the black cutaway jacket and wide-brimmed, low-crowned Stetson, he strapped on his gunbelt and fastened the bottom of its holster to his thigh. After checking that its chamber's nipples were correcly capped, he dropped the long-barrelled, ivory-handled 1860 Army Colt into the holster. With the gun at his side he felt more secure. Folding the dude suit, after slipping the thick wallet into his other coat, he placed it into the grip.

Ready to leave, Derringer sat on the bed and gave thought to his future. He might have stayed on in Mulrooney as floor manager of a gambling house and part-time deputy marshal, but the idea did not appeal to him. Dusty Fog and the floating outfit would soon be headed back to Texas and Derringer felt disinclined to stay longer in the town. So he would travel east on the train until he

found some place offering high-stake gambling
with opponents capable of challenging his skill.

Before Derringer reached any decision on where
he would direct his next activities, he heard a crash
in the room above him. During his time as a
deputy, he had helped burst through enough doors
to recognize the sound. At the first scream he rose,
blew out the lamp and headed for the window
with grip and cane in hand. Overhead the screams
continued, but nothing in their timbre led Derringer to believe other than fear and fury at the in-
trusion caused them.

However, he knew the time for departure had
come. Clearly the deputy had recognized him and,
most probably, had sold that information to the
gang. While Derringer did not know how they had
found him so quickly, he gave the matter no
thought. The first attempt might have failed, but
Nabbes would not allow the matter to rest so easily. Given a chance to examine the register, the little man was smart enough to guess what had
happened. So Derringer must leave the hotel before
the gang boxed him in.

Above him the sound of departing feet faded
away. Shouts of complaint rang through the building, but no shots. Crossing to the side window,
Derringer drew open the curtains and climbed out.

On landing in the alley, he slid free the cane-gun and gripped it in his right hand. As the gang knew his identity, there was no point in attempting to hide the weapon and he might need it in a hurry.

Knowing that the men who had broken into room eighteen would most probably flee the hotel through the more accessible front doors, Derringer discarded the possibility of escape along the street. So he turned toward the rear of the building. At the same moment Throck came around the corner.

Although only intending to investigate the cause of the disturbance—and ensure a clear line of escape should such become necessary—Throck read significance in the sight of Derringer climbing through the window. Despite the bright moon overhead, the alley lay in shadow. For all that, even with the change of clothing, Throck recognized the gambler. Recalling the other's skill with the deadly cane-gun, Throck wasted no time. As he started to charge forward, the burly man dipped his right hand into his jacket pocket and it emerged with fingers through a set of knuckledusters.

Catching the faint glint of metal on his attacker's knuckles, Derringer read its menace correctly. Backed by Throck's powerful muscles, the brass-sheathed fist would tear open Derringer's flesh, tumbling him unconscious to the ground, or in such pain that he would be unable to defend himself.

However, Derringer did not intend to allow that to happen, if he could avoid it. From what he had seen, he believed Ferrely's statement on Throck's ability as a pugilist. Even without the knuckleduster, the big bruiser would make a dangerous opponent in a brawl. Not that Derringer intended to start slugging it out with Throck unless driven to it. The odds against him succeeding in a toe-to-toe fight stood too high to be contemplated. Long before he could beat the big man, always assuming that he might—the men from inside the hotel would arrive and take cards.

Thinking at top speed, Derringer also saw that he would lack the time to turn the cane-gun. Nor would shooting be the answer. He did not know how strong a hold Nabbes might have on the local law, although he doubted if the little man was related to either marshal or justice of the peace. Even should the town marshal be honest and unaware of the gang's activities, he would not take kindly to a shooting in his bailiwick. Derringer did not want to wind up in jail. Even if the court set him free, Nabbes' gang would know where to lay hands on him.

Long before those thoughts reached crystalization, Derringer acted. Swinging forward his left arm, he pitched the grip underhand toward Throck's legs. Letting out a howl as he tripped, the big man stumbled in Derringer's direction. A step into the alley's center carried the gambler clear of the other's reaching hands. Already feet were pounding along the sidewalk at the front of the hotel, so Derringer knew he must not delay in making good his escape. However, he had to slow Throck further before going.

Around lashed the cane, colliding with the big man's rump as he blundered past. Maybe the cane's outer surface was vulcanized rubber treated so that it looked like wood, but underneath lay a barrel of Remington's finest cast-steel. So the cane-gun also made a mighty effective club. It lacked the springy whip-action of a schoolteacher's cane, but carried enough power to send Throck sprawling onward. He landed on hands and knees as the Keeble brothers appeared at the front end of the alley.

"There he is!" Bud screeched, and plunged forward with the same kind of recklessness shown when playing cards.

Too late Bud saw Throck landing before him. Making an attempt to bound over the other, his foot struck Throck's shoulder and he tumbled on top of the big man.

Less impetuous than his brother, Fenn avoided being tripped. He saw Derringer turn after striking Throck, scoop up the grip and dart off toward the rear of the building. However, Fenn knew better than go after the gambler alone, and shared Derringer's aversion to gun-play. So he skidded to a halt and hauled his cursing brother erect.

"How are you, Joe?" Fenn asked.

Horrible obscenities rose as Throck forced himself erect and for a moment he stood glaring as if contemplating an attack on the two brothers. Recognizing the danger, Fenn let out a yell which halted the man and made him aware of their identity. With the danger of attack by their companion ended, Fenn gave the order to get after Derringer.

Although hampered by the cane-gun and bag, the gambler managed to build up a satisfactory lead during the time it took Fenn to untangle the other two. Once clear of the hotel, Derringer decided that his best bet would be to get out of town. On the way in he remembered that the train had come down a steep gradient about a mile from the town. The Eastbound would ascend the slope slowly enough for him to board it. Unless the gang guessed what he planned, he should be able to escape that way. However, first he must lose the trio from the hotel.

Any hopes that he might already have done so ended abruptly as he ran down a deserted residential street.

"There he goes!" yelled Bud's excited voice from behind.

"Get after him!" Throck echoed.

"Hold down that row, damn you!" Fenn snarled, continuing to run. "Do you want to bring the marshal on to us?"

Apparently the others did not, for neither raised his voice again. Instead they concentrated on following the fleeing gambler. Although lamplight glowed at some windows, none of the residents appeared to investigate the noise. Nor did any pursuit appear to have been organized at the hotel.

Knowing that the other men, not carrying anything to slow them down, would be able to keep him in sight, Derringer sought for a way to throw them off his tracks. With that in mind, he darted through an alley between two buildings and entered what appeared to be the headquarters of a well-organized freighting outfit. Several big Conestoga wagons, with their canopies removed, formed a line to his left. A blacksmith's forge and several wooden buildings, only one of which showed lights at its windows, made a rough oblong with a large pole corral in its center. Beneath the heavily leaved branches of a huge old oak tree stood another wagon, its white tarpaulin cover in place.

A number of horses occupied the corral, but Derringer gave no thought to taking one as a means of escape. For one thing they did not look to be saddle-stock, being large, powerful animals bred for hauling wagons. Another, more vital reason was that anywhere west of the Mississippi River horse stealing carried a penalty of death; the punishment generally being administered promptly and without recourse to the legal courts. While only the one cabin showed signs of life, Derringer did not intend to take a chance.

So he started forward, meaning to twist between the buildings in the hope of confusing and eluding his pursuers. The route he took led him toward the covered wagon beneath the oak tree. So far the three men had not come into sight, but he heard the sound of their feet drawing closer.

Then he saw something which momentarily drove all thoughts of the trio from his head. A movement by the lighted cabin caught his eye and he looked in that direction. Coming through the gap between the two buildings, a big dog started to turn on to the cabin's porch. Then it halted, head swinging toward where Derringer had come to a

stop. Feeling the wind behind him. Derringer knew
it must be carrying his scent to the dog. Confirma-
tion came from the animal as it cut loose with a
deep-throated hound-bay and started forward.

Every professional gambler learned to think and
act fast, not only studying the immediate answer to
a problem but also how its solution might affect
the future. He knew that he could not carry out his
original plan with the hound coming for him. Even
if its baying did not bring people from the occupied cabin, the noise would guide the Keebles and
Throck to him. However, although the dog posed
a threat to his safety, it offered him a slender
chance to escape.

Darting to the rear of the wagon, he prepared to
toss his grip and cane underneath. Then he saw
that the rear flaps of the canopy were hanging unfastened and inside stood a number of boxes.
Swiftly Derringer tossed the grip along the top of
the wagon's load and heard it fall to the bed beyond the boxes. Swinging himself up on to the gate
of the wagon, he slid the cane-gun into the gap between the side and the load. Then he hauled himself to the top of the canopy and stood on it.
Already the hound was drawing nearer, its ringing
bugle bawl shattering the night in no uncertain
manner. At the other side, the three pursuers

turned into the alley which led Derringer to the freighter's yard.

Derringer did not remain on the canopy, but swung himself into the branches of the oak. Carefully he eased himself around the trunk, standing on a stout limb concealed by the leaves, but just able to see what went on. Peering downward, he saw the hound—a large bluetick from all appearance—drawing closer. Never, not even when sweating out the draw for a possible straight flush with two thousand dollars of his money in the pot, had Derringer felt such tension. Coming toward the tail-gate of the wagon, the hound slowed down. In a moment it would catch his scent and, if used for the normal kind of hunting after semi-arboreal creatures, work out where he had gone. Then it would rear up on hind-legs against the wagon and send its "treed" song ringing through the night air.

"Come on, you three!" Derringer breathed. "Where the hell are you?"

A larger pool of light glowing drew Derringer's attention to the cabins. He saw two shapes leaving the building and heading toward the hound. Then he turned his eyes back to the dog beneath him. Even as it slowed down, the three men came into sight through the alley. Instead of stopping, the hound acted just as Derringer hoped it might and headed, baying loudly, toward the trio.

In the lead of his companions, Fenn Keebles saw the approaching hound and skidded to a halt. Even the impetuous and truculent Bud stopped abruptly at the sight before him and Throck appeared to be frozen in his tracks. Standing on stiff legs, tail poker-rigid in the air, powerful eighty-pound frame braced in muscle-rippling readiness to spring forward, the big bluetick hound presented a mighty threatening aspect, and one few men would care to risk challenging.

Balancing carefully on the limb and avoiding any movement that might rustle the surrounding foliage, Derringer watched the two figures from the cabin pass beneath him. While the bigger, bulky shape armed with a twin-barrelled shotgun moved forward, his smaller, more slender companion halted against the tree's trunk almost directly below the hidden gambler. Standing there in the shadows thrown by the branches, the second figure held a revolver ready for use and watched the intruders.

"Hey!" yelled Fenn, looking under the tree and not up at its branches as he would if he knew of Derringer's hiding-place. "Call off that dawg, will you?"

"After you've told us what brings you here," the larger figure rumbled in a deep voice, keeping his shotgun aimed hip-high at the trio.

"Get it away, or I'll blow its fool head off!" Bud howled.

"You just try it, son," warned the big man under the tree, "and I'll right soon be doing some 'blowing' on my own account."

"Stand still and keep your blabber closed, Bud!" Fenn ordered, conscious that they offered a clear target out in the open, while the same did not apply to the two shapes under the oak's branches. So he continued in a conciliatory manner. "He's only a fool kid, mister, and don't mean nothing by his talk."

"What're you doing 'round here?" demanded the big man, neither relaxing nor lowering the shotgun.

"A feller tried to rob the Talbot Hotel and we chased him down this ways," Fenn explained. "We figured he'd come through here and followed him, only the dawg stopped us."

"Maybe he's hid in that there wagon," Bud went on, and made as if to move toward the vehicle.

Although the bluetick had fallen silent on hearing the big man's voice, it let out a low, menacing growl which brought Bud to an immediate halt.

"That's better," said the big man. "Ole Bugle here don't let nobody go near my wagons after dark. Which same he'd've stopped that feller you're after had he come through here."

A point which the trio, even Bud, could understand. Remembering where they were, Fenn Keebles looked harder at the shadowy figures beneath the tree. While he could see little of the second shape, other than the fact that it held a gun, Fenn decided that he could identify the big man.

"You'll be Dobe Killem, I reckon, mister," Fenn announced in his most winning manner. "This here's your local depot."

"I'm Killem," confirmed the big man, but his companion still took no part in the conversation.

"You're not often here, that's why we didn't recognize you," Fenn continued. "Say, maybe that feller managed to get to the wagon and hid inside."

"He'd have one helluva tight squeeze to do that afore Bugle got to it from the porch. Even if there was room in back. The wagon's loaded ready for pulling out in the morning."

"There'd not be time for him to do it, Fenn," Throck growled. "He must've come into the alley, then snuck back out again in the shadows so's we missed seeing him go."

"Or gone along the cabin here and out the next

one," Fenn went on. "We'd best get after him. While we stand here jawing, he's putting distance between us."

"Let's go, then!" Bud suggested, seeing his chances of revenge on Derringer fading.

"Hold it!" Fenn snapped urgently, nodding to the watchful hound. "Mind if we get on our way, Mr. Killem?"

"Feel free," the freighter replied. "Leave 'em be, Bugle, Lie down."

Obediently the bluetick stretched itself on the ground. Not until then did Fenn offer to move. Turning, he led his companions off along the alley at a fast walk. Neither Killem nor the other figure beneath the oak spoke until after the sound of the departing trio's footsteps faded away.

"Wonder who they're after?" Killem remarked. "Maybe somebody their bunch've slickered and's going to tell the marshal."

"Could be," replied his companion. "Say, Dobe, I allus allowed that fool Bugle wasn't worth a cuss as a tree-dog."

"How's that?" grunted Killem.

"You can come on down now, feller," the other said, ignoring the question and directing the words toward the branches of the oak. "They're gone and I'd sure admire to know how the hell you got close enough to the wagon to climb up there without ole Bugle getting to you first."

Being a professional gambler taught a man to control his emotions and only show such feelings as he desired others to see. For all that, Derringer could not hold down an involuntary movement in his surprise. In addition to the shock of learning that one of the pair below knew of his presence, something further caused surprise. Maybe the second figure wore male clothing and had acted mighty competently all through the preceding events—but the voice was that of a young woman.

Chapter 4

~~~~~~~~~~~~~~

REALIZING THAT HE WOULD GAIN NOTHING BY IG-
noring the girl's words, Derringer started to climb
around the tree's trunk and down on to the wagon.
Suddenly a low curse broke from Killem and he
moved forward to draw open the canopy's flaps,
then peered inside. Letting the flaps fall together,
the big man withdrew to leave the way clear for
Derringer to descend. The girl walked to Killem's
side, twirling away the Colt Navy revolver with casual, practiced ease. Standing in the open, she and
Killem gave Derringer his first clear look at them.

Although the owner of a large, successful business, Dobe Killem still dressed like a working
freight driver, in buckskin jacket, open-necked

shirt, with pants tucked into calf-high, low-heeled boots. All in all he gave the impression of rugged capability, controlled hardy toughness and being a man who would stand no nonsense. Standing balanced lightly on his feet, he studied Derringer with an air of suspicion only to be expected under the circumstances.

Not that Derringer devoted much attention to Killem, being more intent on confirming his suspicions about the girl. Bareheaded, her mop of short, curly red hair framed a tanned, freckled face that, while not out-and-out beautiful, was good-looking, merry and very attractive. Maybe she wore men's clothing, but a feller would have to be near on blind to imagine it covered a *male* figure. Five foot seven or so in height, the fringed buckskin jacket she wore hung open to still any lingering doubts as to her sex. Under it the tartan shirt clung to her frame, its neck open low enough to show the commencement of the valley between the full swell of her breasts. Like the shirt, her blue jeans—ending in flat-heeled boots—looked to have been bought a size too small and shrunk further in washing. She trimmed down to a naturally slim waist, no corset could hide itself under that shirt, then curved out to rich, well-formed buttocks and shapely legs. Around her middle hung a gunbelt, the Navy Colt's ivory handle turned butt forward in the fast-draw holster. A coiled, long-lashed bull whip was thrust into her waistband at the left side.

Some folks might have thought the girl's appearance a touch bizarre, or regarded her armament as mere ostentation. Derringer did not think of either clothing or weapons in such a light; in fact, he knew them to be anything but that.

"Just keep your hands in plain sight, mister," Killem ordered, swinging his shotgun into line the moment Derringer dropped to the ground and before the gambler could catch his balance. "How'd you manage to get the flaps open afore Bugle got across here?"

"I didn't have to," Derringer replied. "They weren't fastened when I came."

"The hell you say!" snapped the girl. "Is everything all right inside, Dobe?"

"Didn't look to be anything missing," the freighter answered. "But you'd best take a walk up to the house with us, anyways, mister."

Faced by the shotgun, Derringer could raise no objections. Not that he wanted to, being eager to get out of sight in case Throck and the Keebles brothers returned. He felt sure that he could calm the other two's suspicions, but wished to be under cover while doing so.

After the girl had gone to the wagon and lashed down its covers, she joined Killem in herding Derringer toward the cabin. Although it followed them to the door, the bluetick did not enter the building. Instead it settled down on the porch as if used to doing so regularly.

The room Derringer entered looked much like a ranch's bunkhouse, except that harness and bull whips took the place of lariats and saddles on the beds. Coffee bubbled in a pot on the stove, but neither Killem nor the girl offered to pour the gambler a drink. Derringer decided that the time had come to make himself known to his captors. So he grinned amiably at the girl and began:

"If you didn't leave those flaps unfastened——"

"Which I for sure as hell didn't!" she interrupted.

"And I didn't unfasten them," Derringer continued. "That means some person or persons unknown did it."

"That's real smart thinking, mister," Killem put in. "Or would be if ole Bugle hadn't been laid on the porch since nightfall."

"Only he wasn't on the porch when I come through the alley," Derringer replied. "He came from between the cabins across this way just before I got near the back of the wagon."

"Maybe something made him go around the back," the girl remarked.

"He'd not stop away long enough to let anybody sneak in here and unfasten the wagon flaps," Killem objected. "Even if this gent did scare 'em off afore they could steal anything."

"I dunno," the girl said. "He was away for near on a day once."

"That was when he went after some passing pilgrim's bitch!"

"All right, so there's another bitch in heat around catching his eye. You men're all alike when it comes to *that*. You hear anybody pulling out in a hurry as you come through the alley, mister?"

"Nope," admitted Derringer and, considering that he must establish his identity, went on, "Maybe he, the feller who opened the flaps, hid in the possum belly of your wagon—like Belle Starr did when you sneaked her out of Elkhorn."

Surprise showed on the girl's face. "You know Belle?"

"I've never had the pleasure," Derringer replied. "Mark Counter told me about it one night while we were making the rounds in Mulrooney."

Stepping forward, the girl reached out a hand to draw open Derringer's jacket and run a finger down his vest front. With that done, she turned to Killem and gave a nod.

"Pinholes, Dobe. He's worn a badge and if it was with Mark in Mulrooney, I'd say that makes you Frank Derringer, friend."

"I'm Frank Derringer," agreed the gambler, knowing that his reference to the incident with Belle Starr* would convince the girl. "Mark kept allowing that you'd likely be along to Mulrooney visiting, but Cap'n Dusty said we'd enough fuss and trouble on our hands without Calamity Jane showing up."

"All those floating outfit bunch think real high of me," grinned the girl called Calamity Jane. "They just try to hide it."

In many ways, Calamity Jane could claim to be just as much a living legend as Dusty Fog, Mark Counter, the Ysabel Kid and the rest of Ole Devil Hardin's floating outfit, or any other of the Westerners who received acclaim in the Eastern Press. Born Martha Jane Canary, few people would recognize her by that name. As Calamity Jane, she had gained and attracted notice; although some of the stories about her parentage—as daughter of a notable Plains Indian princess—or reason for heading West and becoming a female freight-wagon driver—

---

* Told in *Troubled Range*.

as the beautiful and talented daughter of a wealthy Eastern businessman seeking to forget a dead fiancé—bore little resemblance to the truth.

Wishing to go West and start a new life, Charlotte Canary had left her family in the care of a St. Louis convent. There had been too much of her mother in Martha Jane for her to settle down to such a restricted life. So she ran away, hiding in one of Dobe Killem's west-bound wagons. A variety of circumstances prevented Killem from returning the girl. Regarded as a lucky charm among the drivers, she gained an unconventional education; yet one designed to help her in a new way of life. From the drivers she learned to live off the country, care for, harness and drive a six-horse wagon team, handle firearms with considerable efficiency, use a long-lashed bull whip as an extension of her arm. She picked up a skill in self-defense from the same source. The latter came in useful, for Calamity went into saloons with the other drivers. On occasion the female employees objected to her custom, so Calamity learned to hold up her end in a hair-yanking brawl. Living a healthier life than the average saloon-girl, she had yet to meet defeat at one's hands.* Happy-go-lucky, living each day to the full,

---

* Told in *The Wild Cats,* the story of Calamity's only defeat.

Calamity Jane had won the admiration and friendship of many people. Looking at her, Derringer could imagine why.

Although the introduction calmed Dobe Killem's suspicions, he still felt that the matter called for clarification.

"What's it all about, Derry?" he asked, while Calamity collected the coffee-pot and started to fill cups. "Why were that bunch after you?"

"For robbing the hotel—they said."

"Since when did that bunch of cold-decking, four-flushing pikers start helping the law?" Calamity snorted. "Neb, our straw-boss here, pointed the Keebles out to me in the street yesterday. Allowed them and their bunch fleeced one of our drivers a piece back. That's why I kept quiet about you when I saw who they were. Did they try their game on with you?"

"You might say that," Derringer smiled.

"Way they were acting," Killem put in, "I'd say you won."

"Let's say I was a mite trickier than them," Derringer replied and told the others all about the game.

"Well I'll swan!" chuckled Killem at the end of the recital. "Ain't you the nervy one?"

"Thing being, they'll not give up that easy,"

Calamity stated. "How'd you figure on leaving town, Derry?"

"On tonight's train."

"They'll be watching the depot for you," Killem warned.

"Sure. So I figure to go out of town and jump it on the slope to the east."

"You try that and you're plumb likely to get your head blowed off," Killem said. "Last feller who did it stopped the train for a bunch of his pards to rob it. So now there're guards along with orders to ventilate anybody who tries to jump aboard out there at night."

"Stage, then."

"And the depot's right on Main Street," Calamity pointed out. "Happen that bunch're dead set on getting you, they'll not miss any bets like watching the stage depot. Are you dead set on going East?"

"Not so that I can't change my mind," Derringer admitted. "Do you have a better idea?"

"I'm taking that wagon-load of supplies to Banyan," she replied. "You can come along with me, happen Dobie don't mind—which he don't."

"Is it all right with you, Dobe?" Derringer asked.

"Sure. The other wagons aren't here yet and you

going along'll save me using one of the stable-hands as a shotgun guard."

"You carrying anything important?"

"Just general supplies for a couple of ranches and folks in Banyan," Killem answered.

"Nothing special, then?" Derringer went on.

"Not real special, and nothing like—say a box of gold or money somebody wanted sneaking out to 'em unsuspected."

"Unless you count that box full of decks of cards," Calamity put in.

"Oh yeah, them," Killem said, nodding. "We've shipped some of 'em afore now, gal. They're for a store-keeper in Banyan, he acts as jobber for the company that prints 'em. I'd say that he supplies the whole town from the number of 'em he has sent to him."

"They do allow that there's gambling goes on in Banyan," commented Calamity with an air of wide-eyed innocence that brought a grin to Derringer's lips.

From all Derringer had heard about the town, claiming that gambling went on there was like allowing folks prayed in a church. Although the railroad missed it by some eighty miles, Banyan had grown fast through a number of fortunate circumstances. In addition to being near Fort Brace, which acted as base for two infantry regiments and a force of cavalry, a small but thriving gold-mine business brought men and money to the town. While the buffalo hunters who once formed a large portion of the customers grew less with the shrinking of the herds, cattlemen moved in to utilize the grazing left vacant. In such a boom-town atmosphere gambling could be expected to flourish, and, by all accounts, Banyan offered any kind of action a man might desire. That had been one of the reasons Derringer decided to accept Calamity's offer.

"I'd heard there might be," he assured the girl. "So there'd be nothing on the wagon anybody'd want to steal?"

"If you're still thinking about that back flap being open, any of the load'd sell easy enough could somebody lay hands on it," Killem replied. "Maybe somebody saw Bugle away from the yard and took a chance, only you scared him off afore he could take anything."

"Could be," Derringer admitted.

"Anyways," Calamity stated, "there won't be another chance, Neb'd best put one of the boys to guarding it when they come back from their drinking and carousing in town."

"Drinking and carousing yet," grinned Killem. "A schooner of beer each, a few hands of penny-ante poker and the weekly session of lying about the good old days is all they're doing."

"I can't help it if they're not as young and feisty as they used to be," Calamity sniffed. "Fact being, they never were."

"*Women!*" Killem snorted. "I'll have Neb set a guard. You got any baggage that needs gathering, Derry?"

"I always travel light. What I have's in the wagon. I threw it over the top of the load before I climbed up into the tree."

"You think fast," Killem complimented. "That was a smart play, climbing up into the tree when you saw Bugle. He went underneath you, saw them jaspers and headed to them afore he'd time to get your scent. Then we all thought you couldn't be in the yard."

"Not me," contradicted Calamity. "I was over by the stove when Bugle took to bawling and looked out of the window. So I saw you climb up there."

"And didn't say a word about it," Killem growled.

"You're always telling me us women talk too much," Calamity reminded him, and looked at the gambler. "How about it, Derry. Do you want to come to Banyan with me?"

"I've nothing to go any other place for," Derringer replied. "Sure, I'll go along. Only it'll mean we'll be alone on the trail with each other."

If the thought shocked Calamity, she failed to show it. "Shucks," she said. "I'm game to take a chance on *that* if you are."

Shortly after dawn next morning Calamity drove her wagon out of Tribune. As she passed a livery barn, she saw Bud Keebles and Ferrely coming from it. Resisting the temptation to stop and ask if the trio had caught their man, she continued to drive. For his part, Bud did no more than glance at the girl seated alone on the wagon box and then turned his attention back to his companion. While passing the Wells Fargo office, she saw Throck seated on the porch. Although he looked her over, the burly man gave no sign of suspecting anything.

Once clear of the town, Calamity held her team to a fast walk and allowed them to work off the friskiness caused by rest and grain-feeding. For a mile she concentrated on the team, then as they settled down turned her interest to the back trail. After another half a mile she looped the reins loosely around the brake-handle. Without slowing the team, she turned on the box and unfastened the front of the canopy.

Inside the wagon, a warm-looking Derringer

blinked as light flooded through the open front. When assembling the load, a space had been left at the front in which Calamity could spread her bed at night. Derringer had hidden in that space, with front and rear canopy flaps lashed down, to prevent Nabbes' gang knowing that he was travelling with the girl. Despite having heard nothing to alarm him, the gambler held his cane-gun ready for use.

"Come on out," Calamity suggested. "There's nobody after us."

"Were they watching?" he asked, joining the girl on the box.

"I saw young Keebles and another coming out of the livery barn," she replied. "Likely they'd been asking if you'd got a hoss. And there was that big Throck jasper watching the Wells Fargo stage office. They must want you bad, Derry."

"I can think of near on fifteen hundred right good reasons, Calam."

"Whooee! I'm doing the wrong kind of work. Anyways, they don't know you've come out with me. We'll fool 'em a mite more soon."

A battered U.S. Cavalry *kepi* perched at a rakish angle on Calamity's head and she sported a tight-rolled green bandana knotted around her neck. Seated comfortably on the wagon box, she handled the ribbons of the powerful six-horse team with complete confidence. A Winchester Model 1866 carbine rode in a boot fastened to the side of the wagon in easy reach of her right hand.

"How'd you figure on doing the fooling?" Derringer asked.

"We're not sticking to the Banyan trail. I've some other stops to make. So they'll not know where to find us. I tell you, Derry, there's not a thing to worry about."

Although Derringer felt that the girl might be a touch optimistic, he grew more into line with her thoughts as the day went by. Especially when they left the main trail to follow a winding, narrow track across the range. By nightfall they reached their first delivery point, a small ranch-house, and had seen no sign of pursuit. However, he figured that Nabbes would not allow the matter to rest, nor give up the attempt to find him. There might still be danger.

Seated at the table in the small saloon's back room, Eli Nabbes looked around the circle of faces. Night had fallen and the gang had gathered for a debate.

"It's been two days," he said. "I tell you, Derringer's got out of town."

"Not on any stage, that's for sure," Fenn Keebles stated. "Me and Joe've watched 'em leave and I've followed 'em maybe three mile along the way."

"You've been watching the railroad depot, Eli," Ferrely pointed out. "And had Bud out on that slope in case Derringer tried to jump a train there. And I can't get word of him hiring a hoss."

Knowing his steerer's skill at obtaining information, Nabbes accepted the statement. Before any more could be said, the door opened and the saloon-keeper looked in.

"Billy Bitzer wants a word with you, Eli," he announced.

For a moment Nabbes thought of declining, then he changed his decision. Bitzer was a small-time gambler who hovered on the fringe of actual crime. Possibly he possessed information about Derringer, for Nabbes had passed the word that he would welcome such news.

"Send him in," ordered the little man.

The man who entered wore cheap flashy town clothes and carried himself with an air of cocky assurance, like one who knew he brought news of importance. Throwing a glance at the door, he made no attempt to start speaking until the saloon-keeper had closed it from the other side.

"Got something you might want to hear, Mr. Nabbes," Bitzer started, coming to the table.

Which meant, as Nabbes realized, that money must change hands before he heard the news. However, he also knew that Bitzer would not visit him unless possessing worthwhile information. So he took out his wallet and nodded.

"Tell it then, Billy."

"I don't know all of it," admitted Bitzer, with the air that what he knew ought to be enough. "Only I've been working for Ted Claggert from Banyan for the past few days."

"So?" Nabbes demanded, knowing Claggert to be floor-manager in one of Banyan's leading saloons.

"He didn't pay me all that good," Bitzer remarked pointedly.

Slowly, almost reluctantly and without allowing the other to see how much the wallet held, Nabbes drew a ten-dollar bill into sight and then a second.

"Twenty's all it's worth, and not that unless there's more," he stated.

"There's more," promised Bitzer. "Like how a couple of nights back I got hold of a bitch red-hot in heat for Ted——"

"And?"

"Took it down back of Dobe Killem's freight

yard to lure away that big bluetick that's kept there."

Watching his customer, Bitzer saw just a slight sign of interest. Yet he felt that his words had caught the rest of the gang's notice. It seemed that Bud Keebles meant to say something, but Nabbes glared the youngster into silence.

"Why'd he want you to do that?" the little man inquired.

"So's he'd have time to get in there and change a box that was on a wagon."

"So what's important about *that?*" Nabbes snorted, making as if to replace the money.

"Claggert don't know that I found out what was in the boxes they changed. Decks of playing cards."

"What time'd that be?" Fenn Keebles put in. "When you was making the swap, I mean?"

"I didn't make it. All I had to do was get the bitch, let her go into the alley on a long line and haul her out when the bluetick come sniffing around her. Claggert and his pard done the swap."

"All right, you're clean, innocent and done nothing!" Fenn snorted. "But what time was it?"

"I'd say maybe half after nine," Bitzer answered, wondering what caused the question. "We had to wait until Killem's straw-boss and hands went to the Long Rail so'd there'd only be Killem and

Calamity Jane there and less chance of anybody roaming around."

"How about the hound?" Nabbes said. "How long was it away?"

"I dunno for sure," Bitzer told him. "All I did was lead it off after the bitch a ways, let 'em get tied together and left 'em. It was away long enough for Claggert to do the swap."

Clearly Bitzer felt that he had done his share, for he reached across the table in the direction of the money. However, Nabbes made no attempt to relinquish it.

"You figure that's worth twenty bucks?" the little man demanded. "Whyn't you come and tell us sooner?"

"Hell, Claggert didn't leave until nightfall and kept me with him until just afore he went. I come as soon as I could."

"Why'd you reckon he swapped them boxes?" Throck spoke up for the first time, scowling in a puzzled manner.

"I didn't ask," Bitzer stated. "All I know is that he wanted them changing and without Killem suspecting anything. That's why he didn't let me kill the dog once I got it clear of the yard."

"Here," Nabbes said, sliding the money across the table. "And don't go peddling your news to anybody else. Happen I hear that you do, I'll let Claggert know where I got it."

"I'll keep quiet, trust me," Bitzer replied, knowing what his fate would be if Claggert knew of his treachery. The only reason he remained alive was that the floor-manager did not realize the full extent of his knowledge; or how he had disobeyed orders by leaving the coupled dogs and returning cautiously to a place where he could see into the yard. Having watched the exchange, Bitzer had slipped away and acted as if he had followed Claggert's instructions to the letter.

"What's that all about, Eli?" Ferrely demanded after Bitzer left. "We don't have so much money that you can toss away twenty bucks like that."

"Don't, huh?" Nabbes snorted, although he knew that the other spoke the truth with regard to their financial standing. "What time was it when you boys lost Derringer that night?"

"Coming up to quarter to ten, I'd say," Fenn replied.

"Hell!" Throck ejaculated. "He could've got into the yard with the dog gone and hid in the wagon."

"The dog was there," Bud objected.

"It must've come back after he hid, seen us and made for us," Fenn guessed. "So we figured he couldn't be around."

"We should've searched that damned wagon," Bud growled.

"With Killem and that feller throwing down on us?" Throck scoffed.

"Feller be damned!" Fenn snapped. "That was no feller, it was Calamity Jane. She stood back so we'd not know it was a woman."

"And Calamity Jane's real friendly with Mark Counter from what I've heard," Nabbes breathed. "That means she'd help Derringer if he asked for it."

"Huh! He warn't on the wagon with her when she pulled out yesterday," Bud protested. "I saw her going by."

"That's for sure," Throck went on. "There was just her on the box——"

"Just her!" Nabbes snorted. "Do you reckon Killem'd let her go all the way to Banyan without a guard along, damn it?"

"Maybe not," Throck agreed.

"You could bet your damned life he wouldn't!" Nabbes snapped. "I'll bet Derringer was either hid in the wagon, or waiting outside town someplace for her. Either way he's left town and's headed for Banyan, with our money."

"So what'll we do, Eli?" Fenn inquired.

"Take after him," Nabbes replied. "Lou, go see

if you can find a sucker. We can't leave tonight and could use some extra cash. Comes morning we'll get us some horses and head for Banyan."

"Then what?" Throck wanted to know.

"If Derringer's there, we'll tend to his needings," Nabbes explained. "And if he's not—well, I'll be interested to see what kind of cards they're selling up that ways after Calamity Jane arrives."

Chapter 5

Travelling in Calamity Jane's company proved a novel, entertaining experience and Derringer found it a welcome break from the high pressures of a professional gambler's life. The girl handled her team with a deft competence that many a man might envy. Pulled by six powerful horses bred for such work, the wagon travelled at a good speed even though no longer on the main Banyan trail. By nightfall they had covered some twenty miles and reached a small ranch-house.

"Your gear's at the back here," Calamity told the rancher, after introducing Derringer, and opened the rear end of the canopy.

Although accompanying the girl as a paying pas-

senger, Derringer had already offered to help with
the work. During the stop Calamity made at noon
to rest and feed her team, he had been amused, if
just a touch irritated, by her attitude. Until sure
that he knew sufficient to perform the more menial
routine tasks of caring for her highly prized team
and wagon, she kept a careful watch on him.

Knowing Calamity, Derringer expected to find
the wagon loaded correctly and the consignment of
goods for the ranch placed conveniently at the rear.
So he reached for the nearest box after lowering
the tail-gate, wondering why it seemed both familiar and yet out of place. The box was stoutly made
and securely fastened, bearing the words "BLETCH-
LEY & SONS, 300" on the sides.

"Not that one, Derry," Calamity said. "It's those
decks of cards Dobe told you about. The Tribune
jam-buster* didn't get the damned thing to us until
after all the other gear'd been loaded. He allowed
it'd been put down behind some other stuff and
forgotten."

Given that much information, Derringer remembered where he had seen a similar box. Bletchley &
Sons printed playing cards for a nation-wide mar-
ket and always shipped bulk sales of their stock in

---

* Jam-buster: Assistant yard-master at a railroad depot.

such a manner. Using newly developed techniques of mass-production, the company produced nearly flawless back designs, ensured that all corners be exactly rounded and that no card exceeded the rest of the deck in size by an appreciable amount. Volume of sales allowed Bletchley & Sons to hold the price of their cards down at a competitive level, and the decks could be found in a majority of saloons—Derringer had two new Bletchley decks in his bag, regarding them, as did many gamblers, as the best available.

Setting aside the box, Derringer put it from his mind and helped unload the goods for the ranch.

Moving on the next morning, they travelled across country to the girl's next delivery point. At first Derringer kept watch on their back trail, but by noon on the third day he shared the girl's belief that their ruse had succeeded. Of course, if Nabbes had guessed how he escaped, there might be a reception committee waiting in Banyan. But Derringer saw no way that the little man could know his destination, even if—as Nabbes would by that time—he suspected that Derringer had managed to leave Tribune.

So the gambler felt surprised to see the girl slide her Winchester carbine from its boot on the box. They had made their noon halt and attended to the welfare of the horses. Looking around the rolling, bush- and tree-dotted range, the gambler could see no cause for her action.

"What's up, Calam?" he asked, glancing to where his cane-gun leaned against his seat.

"Nothing," she grinned. "The Banyan trail's down over that next rim. So I likely won't have another chance to shoot a deer for Sam Werner. Neb told me Sam likes a nice young buck brought in with his supplies."

"Need any help?"

"You can come lend a hand to tote it in if I shoot one. Only I'd as soon not leave the wagon without somebody watching it this close to the trail."

"Never was one for crawling around in the bushes, hunting," Derringer grinned. "So I'll stand guard here and come when I hear you shoot."

The division of labor appeared to satisfy Calamity, for she nodded her agreement. Watching the girl head off through the bushes, Derringer grinned. By noon the next day they would be in Banyan and go their separate ways. Knowing Calamity had been quite an experience, although not nearly so hectic as Derringer had expected. According to Mark Counter's stories, the girl possessed the damnedest way of landing herself in trouble.

Among other lessons learned from Dobe Killem's drivers, Calamity had received instructions in living off the country. So she set about hunting for the store-keeper's gift with the same air of competent knowledge that marked most of her activities on the journey. Moving through the bushes on cautious, soft-stepping feet, the carbine held ready to be snapped into her shoulder for a rapid shot, she searched for sign or sound of white-tail deer.

"Damn-fool critters," she mused on finding no tracks, dung droppings or other traces of deer. "Anybody'd think they didn't want me to shoot 'em."

However, she moved on, swinging in a half circle toward the rim above the Banyan trail. Then she came to a halt. From ahead came the slight sound of animals moving, although she could not decide what kind they might be. Advancing stealthily, she passed through the bushes until coming into sight of the sound's source; but she made no attempt to use the carbine. Instead, she studied three saddled horses which stood with their reins tied to the branches of a bush. Tied might be too strong a word, for the reins were merely looped around and not knotted; sufficient to prevent range-trained horses from straying, yet significant when taken with the location and lack of riders.

Anywhere on the open ranges west of the Mississippi River the sight of a riderless horse attracted attention and aroused some concern. Three of them left in such a manner gave a sinister warning. Sufficiently so for a prudent young woman well-versed in the ways of the land to read danger and head to safety. Calamity possessed enough knowledge of the range country to read the message, but could not be termed prudent.

Whoever had brought the horses to that place had left them in a manner that allowed a hurried departure. Scanning the ground, she saw tracks heading toward the rim. Not along it in the direction of her wagon, but going down to the trail. Instead of following the tracks, Calamity walked around the bushes and advanced cautiously to the rim's edge. No matter who owned the horses, be it Nabbes' gang or strangers, she figured seeing them before they became aware of her presence would be the best policy.

Moving over the rim, Calamity found herself compelled by lack of adequate cover to edge along the front of the bushes. Ahead stood a small rock ideal for her purposes and she did not halt until able to lie curled behind it. Looking down at the trail, she saw enough to tell her the precaution had been worth taking. While the men below did not appear to be members of the Nabbes' gang, she doubted if their intentions were harmless or honest.

The trail followed the curve of a valley, disappearing around the other slope about fifty yards from where two men crouched in concealment. At first Calamity saw only the two. Then she located the third, kneeling behind a rock across the trail from his companions. All wore range clothes of a nondescript style, lined rifles toward the curve—and had bandanas drawn up over the lower part of their faces.

That told Calamity all she needed to know. Cowhands riding the drag on a trail drive, or working cattle in sun-dried areas, often drew up a bandana to keep dust from clogging their nostrils. Done for such a reason it attracted no interest, except maybe the thought that somebody had a right smart idea for making life more comfortable.

However, the trio watching the trail were not working among hoof-churned dust. So the position of their bandanas told a different, less innocent story. Outlaws waiting for a victim often masked themselves in that manner. Doing so hid the features and lessened the chances of being recognized, while drawing down the bandana turned it in a split-second from a mask into an ordinary piece of neck-wear.

Men did not crouch in cover, armed with rifles, alongside a trail, with faces hidden behind masks, unless they had good—or real bad—reasons.

Even as Calamity located the third man, but before she could decide what action to take, the sound of approaching hooves reached her ears. Down below, the third man signalled to his companions and waved a hand in the direction of the hoofbeats. Immediately all three settled their rifle butts firmly against shoulders, telling Calamity that they prepared to deal in some way with the rider.

Turning her head, Calamity looked along the trail at the rider who came into view around the curve. Seated on a big black horse, he made an impressive sight. Even from her place the girl could guess his height to be over the six-foot mark and notice the spread to his shoulders. A costly black Stetson, its band decorated by silver discs, sat on shoulder-long dark hair. At that distance Calamity could make out little of the man's face, other than its flowing moustache, due to the shadow thrown by the hat's brim. Not only the hat hinted at wealth. He wore a white linen shirt of elegant cut, string tie, fancy vest. Gray trousers, with sharp creases, tucked into shining riding boots. Around his waist hung a gunbelt of polished leather. An ivory-handled Remington Beals Army revolver pointed butt forward in a contoured holster and hung just right for a fast draw. Between his knees, a magnificent Meanea Cheyenne roll-saddle's fancy stamping and silver decoration further pointed to wealth. He rode lightly despite his size; but clearly did not suspect that he headed into danger.

Calamity knew that cutting in on the game could prove mighty dangerous. The trio were certain to take exception to her interfering in their business. Also, if the rider proved to be skilled enough with his gun to drive off the trio, Calamity was in a position between them and their means of escape. Even given time to think of the risks, she would not have allowed either contingency to worry her.

"Look out, mister!" she yelled, cradling the carbine against her shoulder, sighting and squeezing off a shot at the man on the far side of the trail.

Give him his due, fancy-dressed and long-haired though he might be, the big newcomer knew a warning when he heard it. Nor did he waste time in idle speculation. At the girl's first word, he hauled back on the black's reins. Feeling the sudden tug at its mouth, the spirited horse threw back and turned its head to one side. Doing so saved its master's life. Three rifles cracked almost at the same moment. Both bullets from the men on Calamity's side of the trail flew true; too true. Instead of tearing into the victim's broad chest, they drove into the horse. Head-shot and with a broken neck, the animal went down kicking its last. Although the third man also fired, he missed. The instant before he applied the final pressure to the trigger, Calamity's bullet sliced the air just above his head. Startled by the hissing crack of the girl's lead, he flinched and sent his bullet harmlessly by its intended target.

Feeling his horse go down, the big man kicked his feet from the stirrups and quit its back. Again he showed a knowledge of how to act in such an emergency. While dropping to the ground, he turned his right hand palm outward to twist the Remington from its holster. He landed on the trail, sinking down behind the collapsing horse to keep its body between himself and the rifles.

Showing a remarkable lack of caution, one of the pair below Calamity started to rise for a better view of their victim. To add to his folly, he was still working the lever, ejecting the empty case ready to feed another bullet into the breech. Coming up from behind the dead horse, the big man lined his revolver. An instant before the attacker could reload, the deep bark of the Remington rang out.

Jerking as if struck by an unseen fist, the ambusher's rifle tilted away from its target. Blood began to dribble out of the hole which miraculously appeared between the man's eyes, staining his bandana mask. Spinning around, he dropped the rifle and then crashed forward to hang on the bush behind which he had hidden on his mission of murder.

After shooting, the big man sank rapidly behind the horse and did not even remain long enough to see if he had hit or missed. Nor did he go down a moment too soon. The second man slammed home his Winchester's lever, sighted and fired hurriedly. Taken in haste or not, the bullet sent the expensive Stetson spinning from the victim's head before he disappeared from sight.

Calamity sent two more shots downward without results, other than to prevent the third of the ambushers taking a more active part in the affair. Despite its manufacturer's claims, the weak twenty-eight grain load of the Winchester .44 bullet lacked accuracy at all but close range, especially when used in the short-barrelled carbine. Almost a hundred and fifty yards separated the girl from the farthest man and she knew only luck would give a hit when snap-shooting at that distance.

Turning without exposing himself to the man

behind the horse, the second of the trio scanned the slope for their unexpected attacker. On locating Calamity—without being aware of her sex or who she might be—the man realized that she cut them off from the horses. Aware that the ambush had gone wrong, he knew they must get away. The presence of the unknown shooter up the slope ruled out any chance of them completing their work at that time.

With that in mind, the man took aim and touched off a shot. Behind Calamity, spooked by the shooting, the three horses tore free their reins and bolted. Before the girl could even turn to look, she found troubles of her own. Lead smashed into the ground just ahead of her, erupting dirt into her face. Letting out a cry of shock and pain, she tossed the carbine involuntarily from her. Womanlike, her main concern at that moment was discovering the extent of damage her features had suffered. Tears blinded her, but her instincts told that she had sustained no serious injury.

"Beat it!" yelled the man, seeing Calamity discard her carbine. Then he rose and started to dart up the slope.

Seeing the other's departure, the third man wasted no time. While not sure how badly the attacker on the rim might be hurt, he could see she no longer held the carbine. That left only their victim to contend with. Over fifty yards separated them, long range for a revolver against a fast-moving target. With that idea in mind, the last attacker left concealment and sprinted toward the trail. Already his remaining companion was fleeing upward to where the horses waited and he did not want to be left behind.

The big man saw his third attacker rise and guessed the other's intentions. To stand up and take aim would offer the masked jasper too good a target, one he would not overlook even in flight. So the attempt must not be made that way. Yet the would-be victim had no desire to allow the killing of his horse to go unpunished. Swiftly he wriggled up until, half kneeling behind the body of his mount, he could get the most out of his Remington. Having a strap above the cylinder allowed the revolver to offer a groove rear-sight for aimed shooting, as opposed to a V-shaped nick in the tip of the hammer on the open-framed Army Colt. So the Remington possessed a greater potential for deliberate shooting, a fact the man proceeded to use to his advantage.

Resting both wrists on the saddle and supporting his right hand with the left, he peered along the barrel and squeezed the trigger. Twice the Remington barked without result, the man deftly cocking its hammer on the recoil. Although he heard the lead whistle by, the third man neither stopped nor attempted to use his rifle. On the next crack of exploding powder, he felt a shocking impact and knew he was hit. Snarling through the roaring pain that filled him, he swung to face the big man. Even as the wounded ambusher tried to lift his rifle, the Remington spat again. Caught in the chest by the .44 bullet, he stumbled back a pace or two, dropped his weapon and sprawled on to the trail.

Awareness of the desperate danger she faced drove through Calamity's concern for her features. Quickly she rubbed at her eyes, trying to clear them. Although still half blind with stinging tears caused by the dirt, she saw the second of the attackers coming her way. Flame lanced from his rifle's barrel as he saw her staring at him; but he shot on the run and from the hip, conditions not conducive to careful aiming.

The sight and sound spurred Calamity into thoughts of defense and she immediately saw the difficulty of making any. When she had discarded the carbine, it had rammed its muzzle into the earth in falling. Not deeply, but still enough to cause her grave concern. If the barrel should be clogged with dirt and she sent a bullet along it, the back blast could burst the barrel; or she might wind up picking the breech's piston pin out of her back teeth. Nor would she be given time to check if the Winchester were safe to fire.

Seeing that Calamity had not been seriously injured by his bullet and could now focus her eyes on him, the man realized his danger. Not more than fifteen yards separated them and at that range she could make a hit with the carbine. So he skidded to a halt and whipped the rifle to his shoulder with the intention of drawing a bead on the girl and getting his shot in first. For a moment indecision froze Calamity as she tried to make up her mind whether to chance using the carbine or make a grab for her Colt.

Then a shot cracked from farther along the rim, its bullet churning into the ground below the masked man. Both he and Calamity turned their heads to see who had cut into the game.

On hearing the first crack of Calamity's carbine, Derringer remembered her instructions. Taking up his cane-gun more as a precaution than for any other reason, he prepared to go and help her bring in the trophy. Then the sound of more shooting reached his ears. Not just the carbine, but rifles and a revolver. So he wasted no time in heading toward the noise.

Coming to the top of the rim, he saw enough to recognize Calamity's predicament. Yet he was too far away to do anything effective. While skilled enough with his Army Colt in normal gun-fighting conditions, he lacked the ability to use a hand-gun over the hundred and fifty yards or more that separated him from the girl's attacker. While the cane-gun could not be termed a long-range weapon either, he figured it offered him a better chance than the revolver.

Moving out into plain view, Derringer raised the cane-gun as if it was a rifle. However, despite its twenty inches of barrel, the lack of a butt or adequate sights prevented it from being as accurate as a shoulder arm. The tip of the cocking-spring catch made a rear sight of sorts, but there was no front sight. So all he could do was take a rough aim, press the trigger stud and hope for the best. Doing so diverted the man's attention and put Derringer into danger.

As the masked man saw Derringer begin to reload, he knew the other held a single-shot weapon of some kind. So the next shot might be more accurate unless he prevented it. Up that close he could see Calamity was a woman and reckoned that she posed less of a threat than the newcomer.

So he started to swing the rifle in Derringer's direction.

Unlike the masked man, Calamity knew what kind of gun the gambler held. Aware of the risk Derringer was taking, she knew what she must do. His intervention had given her the brief respite she needed to make up her mind. Ignoring the carbine, she sent her right hand twisting back around the butt of the Colt and slid it from its holster.

"Drop it, feller!" she yelled.

Turning his head at the words, the man became aware that Calamity formed a far more serious threat than he first imagined. Sufficient for him to know he must chance another try by Derringer while he dealt with her. So he turned, swinging the Winchester smoothly at its new target with his forefinger curled ready around the trigger. He moved so fast that Calamity did not have time to shoot and flame licked from the rifle's barrel.

Calamity rolled over and away from the rock, missing death by scant inches as the man's bullet whistled over her body. Striking the rock behind her, it sent a scattering of chips flying and she felt some of them patter against her shirt. Then she landed on her stomach once more and knew she did not dare waste another second. Already the rifle's lever was blurring downward, flicking the empty cartridge case into the air. When it closed, there would be another bullet in the breech and the man was unlikely to miss a second time at so short a range.

Cocked on the draw, Calamity's Colt seemed to line on the man of its own volition. Yet she paused the brief split-second necessary to make sure of her aim before squeezing the trigger. Powder burned inside the revolver's uppermost chamber and a conical .36 bullet curled its way through the rifling grooves of the barrel. Calamity shot the only way she dare under the circumstances. While the rifle's ejected case still rose into the air, before the lever could snap closed, Calamity's bullet flew true to its mark. A blue-rimmed hole sprouted between the man's eyes and turned red as blood began to flow. Going limp, his hands released the rifle. For a moment he remained erect, then he toppled backward to the ground.

Chapter 6

Smoke dribbled from the barrel of Calamity's Colt as she rose to her feet. She cocked back the hammer, tense and ready to shoot again should it be necessary. One glance at the sprawled-out figure told her that the need for further action would not arise. Always a practical young woman, reared in the hard school of frontier life, she knew there had been no way to avoid what she did. In his eagerness to reach where he thought the horses stood waiting, the man would not have hesitated to kill her. So she felt only a slight twinge of regret at ending his life.

Carefully lowering the hammer to rest on the safety notch between two of the cap nipples on the cylinder, she returned the Colt to its holster and looked around her. Derringer ran toward her along the top of the rim, striding out fast with his cane-gun held ready for use. Down on the trail, the big man rose from behind his horse and raised his hand in a wave of thanks. Walking around the dead animal, he approached his second victim, knelt and drew down the masking bandana. After looking at the exposed face, he straightened up and went to where the other body hung on the bushes. Lowering it to the ground, he repeated the inspection. With that done, he threw a regretful glance at his horse, and holstered his Remington.

"Are you all right, Calam?" Derringer gasped, coming to a halt at her side and looking at her with concern.

"Sure," she replied.

"I thought he'd hit you when I saw you drop the carbine."

"Naw. The bullet threw dirt into my face's all. Only when I dropped that fool gun, the barrel likely got plugged and I couldn't chance using it."

Further explanation being unnecessary to any-body who knew "sic 'em" about firearms, Calamity gave none. Walking forward, she picked up the carbine. By chance she was stand-ing with her back to the man who climbed the slope as she inspected the little Winchester. Sure enough sufficient dirt had entered the muzzle to make the discharge of a bullet dangerous to the user. Without Derringer's intervention, Calamity knew she could never have drawn and shot in time to save herself. She figured that whatever her life might be worth, she owed that much to the gambling man.

"Damn it, Calam," Derringer grinned. "If ole Mark wasn't right about you licking all be-jeezus at finding trouble."

"I'm just talented, I reckon," she answered.

"Thanks, young feller," said a deep voice from behind the girl. "You saved my hide there. Did they get you?"

Despite the words, Calamity realized they must be directed to her. So she turned to face the speaker and grinned broadly.

"Nary a scratch," she assured him.

The sight of Calamity and realizing that she was a girl brought the man to a halt. His eyes bugged out a mite as they roamed over her from head to foot, taking in her various unmasculine attributes. Then he flung back his head and let out a bellowing roar of laughter.

"Well I'll swan!" he said, slapping a hand against his thigh. "Folks'll allow I'm getting old for certain sure if they hear that Sultan Banyan mistook *you* for a feller!"

Calamity and Derringer exchanged glances at hearing the name, for both recalled mention of a man called Sultan Banyan. Probably each of them possessed details that the other did not.

Having served with the Union Army during the War between the States, Derringer remembered how Banyan had achieved some fame among supporters of the North. Possibly seeking for a name to counter the fame gained by Dixie's trio of highly successful military raiders—Turner Ashby, John Singleton Mosby and Dusty Fog—the Unionist newspapers invested the colorful Captain "Sultan" Banyan with a greater acclaim than he deserved. Sure he did well on the Kansas–Missouri battle-front, but not in comparison with any of the three Confederate officers. Derringer recalled one incident, that which brought Banyan into public prominence yet also became the center of much controversy.

In addition to knowing the generally accepted facts of Banyan's military career, Calamity was aware that he had been founder of the town which bore his name. According to Killem's Tribune straw-boss, Banyan ran the best, fanciest saloon in town. The name "Sultan" came, according to legend, from his success with women. Studying Banyan's powerful frame and handsome face, she concluded that when younger he could have been the Good Lord's answer to what a gal dreamed about on long, cold winter nights. However, the years, plus good living and maybe dissipation, had left their marks in a slight puffiness of his features and thickening at the waist.

Only for a moment did Banyan stand showing his surprise at learning an attractive girl rescued him. Then he went to the last body, drew down the bandana and exposed the features.

"Know him?" Calamity asked as she and Derringer looked at the dead face.

"Can't say that I do, gal," Banyan answered. "Should I?"

"I dunno," the girl admitted. "What do you reckon they was after?"

"Those masks weren't worn for trick-or-treat at Hallowe'en," the big man grunted. "I'd say they were owlhoots fixing to rob me."

"Not that one," Derringer objected, wondering what prompted the girl's question. "Leastways, the last time I saw him, he was taking pay as one of the guns in a railroad right-of-way fuss."

"A hired gun, huh?" Calamity put in, sounding interested and as if that helped explain matters.

"So?" Banyan demanded. "That kind'd rob their own mothers was they short of cash."

"Have you seen what he's carrying in his pockets?" Calamity asked.

Wondering what lay behind the girl's comments, Derringer moved forward and searched the man. While a deputy in Mulrooney, the gambler had learned where to look for hidden money. He extracted only a few dollars in change from the man's pockets, but a hidden pouch inside the gunbelt yielded a wad of bills.

"A hundred bucks," he told the others after counting his find. "What's up, Calam?"

"Way I saw it, those three aimed to kill this gent as he rode up."

"Anybody'd know the only way they could rob Sultan Banyan'd be after I was good and dead," Banyan stated, yet a slight furrow crept on to his brow.

Something about the big man made Calamity's back hair rise. In addition to addressing her with an air of condescension, he gave the impression that he expected her to wet her pants through sheer delight at being in his presence. So she determined to force her point.

"And nobody'd want you dead bad enough to hire it done?" she asked.

"Not me, gal," Banyan boomed, still in that irritating manner. "I get on *real* well with everybody. Not even any of my four wives'd want to see me dead."

Despite her annoyance, Calamity could not hold back the question which sprang to her lips.

"You've had *four* wives?"

"Had 'em?" Banyan answered, letting out that same bellow of laughter. "I've still got 'em. Why do you think they call me 'Sultan'?"

Noticing how Calamity was glaring at Banyan, Derringer decided that he must intervene. At any moment the girl's volatile temper might boil over, caused by the big man's attitude of masculine superiority. Although not a feminist in the accepted form of the word, she figured that her capabilities entitled her to be treated as an equal and to have her views on the matter in hand respected.

"Did you search the other two, mister?" the gambler asked.

"I looked at 'em and didn't know 'em," Banyan answered.

"Did you search them?" Derringer repeated.

"There wasn't any need that I could see."

"How about taking a look?"

"Why?" Banyan asked.

"Happen they've got as much money on 'em as

this jasper, I'd say they fixed to do more than just rob you," Derringer explained. "Like I said, he's a hired gun. Not top-grade, but good enough to find enough work to stay off the owlhoot."

"Maybe," Banyan said, then looked at the cane-gun in Derringer's hand and Colt at his side. "Say, that wasn't a bad piece of shooting you did, dropping this jasper from back there with a hand-gun.

Having been fully occupied in dealing with the third attacker, Banyan had failed to see how the girl had handled the second. When he looked around him after killing the escaping man, Banyan saw Derringer running along the rim. Finding that Calamity was a girl, he concluded the gambler must have shot the second ambusher from long distance to save her.

"I didn't get him," Derringer corrected. "Calam here dropped him as he come for her."

"Calam——?" Banyan said, looking from Derringer to the girl.

"It's short for Martha Jane Canary, mister," she informed him coldly. "Which same's long for what folks mostly call me—Calamity Jane."

"And let's see you grin *now,* you smug son-of-a-bitch!" she thought after completing the introduction.

Much to the girl's satisfaction, the air of superi-

ority and condescension left Banyan's face. Up to
that point he had regarded her as no more than a
naïve country girl dressed in male clothing to avoid
attracting attention—possibly because she was
eloping with the gambling man and feared pursuit
by her parents. So he had discounted her comments as being an attempt to appear worldly-wise.

In view of the name she gave, he dropped his
eyes to her gunbelt, having overlooked it earlier in
favor of studying the more interesting aspects of
her appearance. His eyes took in the contoured,
well-designed lines of the holster and how the belt
hung just right. Nor did the girl exhibit any self-
consciousness in wearing the rig, or give the impression that it was a mere decoration to aid the
deception of the clothes.

Which meant she was likely talking the truth
about her identity. What was more, he knew that
Calamity Jane probably possessed enough knowledge to draw accurate conclusions from what she
saw. So he would be advised to at least investigate
the matter further. Being Sultan Banyan, he could
not bring himself to an outright admission that he
might be wrong.

"Well I'll swan!" he said admiringly, eyeing the
girl with fresh interest. "And I thought—— So
you're Calamity Jane."

"There's only the one," she replied modestly.

"Some folks I've met've been known to say that's at least three too many," Derringer remarked. "How about it, do we search them?"

"Let's go take a look." Banyan agreed. "If somebody's trying to get me killed, I'd like to know who."

"Most folks would," Calamity said, starting to walk down the slope.

"Just how'd you come to be on hand so helpful, Calam?" Banyan inquired, dropping the overfamiliar "gal," as he followed on the girl's heels.

"We've camped back there and I'd come out to see if I could shoot me a whitetail. Then I found three hosses and figured to see why they'd been left. Soon as I saw them jaspers' masks and you riding up, I allowed I'd best take cards."

"Which I'm right pleased you did," the big man said, then turned his eyes toward Derringer with a question in them.

"I wanted the buck, not him," Calamity stated, before the gambler could tell why he had remained in camp and left the hunting to her. "This here's Frank Derringer, mister."

"Call me 'Sultan,' Calam," boomed Banyan, and once more gave the gambler his attention. "Frank Derringer, huh?" Clearly he considered

Calamity's explanation satisfactory. "Are you still wearing a badge for Dusty Fog?"

"Not anymore. Dusty's finished his work in Mulrooney and's headed back home to Texas."

Banyan regarded Derringer in a more friendly and charitable light on learning his identity. In addition to bearing a reputation as a straight and capable gambler, Derringer had served as a deputy under Dusty Fog. Any man who wore a badge for the Rio Hondo gun-wizard packed sand to burn and could be relied on, in range terms, to take no sass but "sasparilla" from his fellows.

"If you're looking for work in Banyan——" the big man began.

"I'm not, unless I go broke," Derringer interrupted. "All I want's to find a game and lose my pay."

"That you'll find easy enough," Banyan promised. "You can find any sort of game you crave in my town."

Further conversation was prevented by their arrival at the bush where the second body lay. While Banyan searched the pockets, Derringer studied the face.

"Well?" asked the big man.

"Can't say I've ever seen him," Derringer admitted, and nodded to the wad of money Banyan found. "But he's carrying around as much as the other."

Going to the last body, Banyan started to check it over. Once again he brought to light a similar amount of money. To Derringer, keen student of human emotions, it seemed that the big man looked less certain in the face of the proof. Yet Banyan still hesitated to accept the possibility that somebody might want to have him killed.

"So they're carrying money," Banyan said. "Maybe they're greedy and wanted some more."

"Could be," Derringer answered. "Only this jasper fought in that right-of-way war. I'd say whoever hired 'em gave 'em travelling money in case anything went wrong and they'd get the rest when they brought proof they'd earned it."

"Why the masks if they aimed to kill me?"

"This here's a well-used trail," Calamity pointed out. "If anybody saw 'em while they were shooting or getting away, it'd look like they was only owl-hoots."

"And they'd sure as hell not want *you* to know their faces happen anything went wrong," Derringer continued, making an argument he felt sure would appeal to Banyan's ego.

It worked. The big man gave a nod of agreement and said, "That's for sure. They'd know there'd be no living on this earth with Sultan Banyan riled and hunting for their scalps."

"Now we've got 'round to figuring they was after *your* scalp," Calamity said dryly. "I'd reckon we ought to start asking who wants it."

"Hell, Calam," objected Banyan. "Everybody gets on with me."

The glance Calamity directed at the body between them spoke louder than any words. Not wanting Banyan to retreat into the original robbery theory, Derringer offered a possible type of suspect.

"How about the other saloon-keepers in town?"

"There's only Edgar Turnbull's Big Herd that comes close to the Harem and enough trade for all of us."

"Maybe this Turnbull's a hawg," suggested Calamity.

For a moment thought lines furrowed Banyan's brows, but he kept whatever struck him to himself. Yet Derringer formed the impression that the big man had suddenly recalled somebody who might be willing to pay for his death.

"You got a saddle hoss along that I could borrow, Calam?" Banyan asked.

"Nope——"

"You allowed there were three belonging to this bunch up there."

"The shooting spooked 'em so they broke and run," the girl explained. "I can take you in on the wagon, but it'll be tomorrow noon at the earliest afore we hit town."

"Thanks, I'll come. If we're lucky somebody might come along with a hoss I can borrow. Anyways, if I show up later than expected, somebody may let something slip. All I want's a start and I'll do the rest."

"Best get your gear off your hoss," Calamity said. "Then we'll haul it off the trail."

"Yeah," agreed Banyan. "Damn it. When I learn who hired these three I'll break every bone in his lousy body. That was a real good hoss."

"How about the bodies?" asked Derringer.

"There's room in the back of the wagon," Calamity replied, showing no great eagerness.

"Naw," Banyan growled. "We'll leave 'em out here and Tyler Kitson can come collect them. He's town undertaker and can use the trade."

Knowing how the bodies would start to stink, neither Calamity nor Derringer raised any objections. There were goods on the wagon which could be spoiled by the stench of death seeping into them. So, while the girl fetched up two of her team and harness, the men moved the bodies from the trail. A covering of branches, with the bandanas which served for masks tied on and left flapping in the breeze, would serve to keep away coyotes, turkey vultures or other scavengers until the Banyan undertaker and local law could collect them.

With all the removals made, Calamity and the two men returned to the wagon and made ready to move on. Sitting on the box, Banyan dominated the conversation and seemed determined to impress the girl. He proved to be an interesting travelling companion, although his main topic appeared to be Sultan Banyan. For all that he spoke mainly of his achievements, Banyan contrived to avoid being as boring or offensive as most people sound when discussing themselves.

After describing his adventures during the War and since, including how he had watched the town bearing his name grow and prosper, Banyan turned and grinned at the girl.

"I tell you though, Calam," he said. "This's the first time I've ever been saved by a gal. Mostly it's the other way around."

"You save them—or they have to be saved from you?" Calamity grinned.

"A bit of both, only most times they'd as soon not be saved from me," chuckled the big man. "One time I even rescued a genuine Russian countess."

"In Russia?" asked the girl.

"Nope, I've not been out of these United States yet; although I'm fixing on taking a vacation in Europe real soon. It was back on the Missouri border in the War. She'd come out with her husband, fixing to see what went on. Only a bunch of reb Bushwhackers jumped 'em, killed all their army escort and carried them off. My outfit found the bodies and we took up the trail. We found the Bushwhackers' camp and I snuck in that night, settled their guards and stood by them Russians until my boys attacked and run the rebs off."

While the story had been true enough, Derringer noticed that Banyan had omitted to mention one puzzling aspect of it. When captured, the Russian military observer Count Kotchubez and his wife had in their possession a box containing their considerable travelling expenses and a quantity of very valuable jewellery. Although the couple were saved, the box had never been recovered. According to Banyan's story, as Derringer recalled it, the outnumbered rescuers found time only to free the prisoners before being driven off by the main body of the Bushwhackers. Later a strong force of Union cavalry trapped the Bushwhackers, killing many and taking the remainder captive. Rigorous questioning of the survivors failed to produce the Russians' treasure. Nor could the Count and Countess shed light on the matter, for the box had been taken from them by the Bushwhackers' leader. Despite protracted searching of the camp area, the money and jewellery never did come to light.

Naturally such an event caused a stir, but the War was drawing to a close, and soon word of Lee's surrender at the Appomattox court-house gave the soldiers other things to consider. Being concerned with the business of returning to civilian life, Derringer all but forgot the Kotchubez treasure until Banyan's story recalled it to his mind.

Not that Derringer asked questions, for Banyan had gained a reputation as being real touchy on the subject. There had been rumors of enlisted men receiving beatings, and Banyan had killed another officer in a duel over comments made on his knowing where the money and jewellery might be.

After answering Calamity's question about how the Countess reacted to the rescue, Banyan went back to the subject of his proposed holiday in Europe. From hints the big man put out, the girl concluded that he was seeking a female travelling companion. Being a sensible young woman, Calamity made it clear that she had neither desire nor intention to leave her native land.

The subject lapsed and they continued on their

way. At sundown, having made less distance than
expected due to the attempted ambush, Calamity
halted her team on the Banyan side of the Smoky
Hill River's South Fork. As the other side had a
thick coating of woodland along its banks, she
would normally have watered the team and pushed
on for a time before making camp. With night
coming on and no desire to handle her team's welfare in the dark, she contented herself with crossing the ford and halted on the edge of the trail at
the other side. With the men's help, she performed
her chores and then they settled down for the
night. Calamity slept in the back of the wagon,
Derringer underneath it. Claiming that he was
prone to rheumatism, Banyan made his bed—using
blankets borrowed from Calamity's supply—by
the side of the fire.

Before going to sleep, Derringer's last thoughts
were on the Kotchubez treasure, but he formed no
conclusions as to its whereabouts.

Chapter 7

DAWN'S GRAY LIGHT CREPT INTO THE EASTERN SKIES
as Derringer woke. Looking across at the fire's
dead embers, he saw Banyan still lying under the
blankets with the bullet-holed Stetson tilted on his
head. Slight noises sounded above Derringer, then
the wagon shook a little and Calamity swung herself to the ground.

"Morning, Derry," she greeted and nodded to
the fire. "Looks like ole Sultan's not used to getting
up at the crack of dawn."

"I'm not what you'd call real keen on it myself,"
Derringer admitted. "Only I've got used to it recently."

With that he crawled from beneath the wagon.

Sleeping on the ground had not called for much undressing, so all Derringer had removed the previous night was hat, gunbelt and boots. He drew on the boots before emerging, but still held the gunbelt in his hands preparatory to strapping it on. For her part Calamity was dressed, in the western sense, with gunbelt about her middle, holster tip tied to her thigh and the coiled whip rode in its usual place.

"Leave your bed until we've ate," Calamity suggested.

"Su——," Derringer began.

"Toss the belt under the wagon, tinhorn!" barked a voice from the woods across the river.

Despite the shock he received, Derringer made no sudden moves. Yet he also hesitated to obey the command, for he recognized the voice. More than that, Calamity stood in a position where she could see beyond the gambler and she gave a soft-spoken warning.

"Best do it, Derry. It's Nabbes and some of his bunch. They've two rifles lined on you."

Much as obeying went against the grain, Derringer could do nothing but comply. Bucking the odds at that moment would be fatal. So he tossed his gunbelt under the wagon, watching it land on the blankets alongside his cane-gun. Then slowly, keeping his hands in plain sight, he turned to look in the speaker's direction. One glance told him that the situation was not as bad as he expected—it was a whole heap worse.

All but Ferrely of the gang stood among the trees. Throck and Fenn Keebles lined Winchesters, Bud held his Colt, but Nabbes stood with empty hands. When they saw Derringer obey, the men advanced. Even while wading over the ford, they gave no sign of losing the drop. However, Nabbes spoke again as they came ashore.

"Get rid of the gunbelt, Calamity."

"Go to hell!" the girl answered.

"We've no quarrel with you," Nabbes pointed out. "All we want's the tinhorn."

"He's riding my wagon same's the load," Calamity replied.

"Which's why I'm telling you to take off the gunbelt and drop it," Nabbes said evenly, knowing that the girl might try to defend her passenger unless disarmed. "Use your left hand to unbuckle it and move slow."

"Who's the feller by the fire?" Fenn put in.

"Just some drifter I picked up yesterday," Calamity answered, wondering if Banyan would wake in time to help.

"Go wake him, Joe," ordered Nabbes and

turned to the girl, his voice taking on a harder tone. "I'm not asking again."

"Do it, Calam!" Derringer advised. "All they want's their money, then they'll pull out."

Yet he knew that he lied. Maybe Nabbes would be content with just retrieving their losses. Possibly Fenn might want no more, or restrict his revenge to a fist-beating. Most likely Throck had no thoughts on the matter, being willing to follow Nabbes whichever way the little man went.

That left Bud. The youngster's face showed his intentions. Still smarting under the knowledge that his folly had caused the trouble, blaming Derringer for his humiliation, Bud meant to leave the gambler dead. Nothing less would satisfy the young man's bruised ego. However, Derringer wanted Calamity unarmed, so that she would not be tempted to make a foolish play.

Giving a shrug, the girl obeyed the order. Using her left hand only, she unfastened the holster's pigging thong, then unbuckled the belt. With a resigned expression, she swung the belt so that it fell beyond Derringer and away from the wagon. Coming back, in what appeared to be an accidental manner, she freed the whip's lash and sent it behind her, straightening along the ground as it fell.

All the time, Nabbes and the Keebles brothers drew closer.

"I've been waiting for this!" Bud snarled, starting to raise his Colt.

Lying by the dead fire, Banyan appeared to be asleep. Yet he was watching from under his hat's brim. Having woken up just too late to make some effective move, he remained still to await his chance. From what he heard, the newcomers seemed to want Derringer. Why, Banyan could not guess. If the other had been a known card cheat the answer would have been obvious, but Derringer's reputation was good.

One thing Banyan did know. He must do what he could to help. Unless he misjudged Calamity, she would not stand by to see her passenger robbed or abused. Even if he did not owe the girl a debt for saving his life, a sense of chivalry would have made him cut in on her behalf.

Like Derringer, Banyan read Bud's intentions. When the youngster committed a cold-blooded murder, his companions dare not leave behind living witnesses. Which meant that the quartet posed a threat to Banyan's life.

Never given to deep thinking, Throck paid no attention to the manner in which Banyan was dressed. Not that he could see the other's clothing for the blankets, but the hat and saddle used as a pillow should have struck him as being mighty expensive items in the possession of a mere drifter picked up on the trail.

Walking up, his rifle held slanting toward the blanket-draped figure, Throck kicked Banyan in the ribs with enough force to bring a grunt of pain.

"Ge——!" he began.

Like a flash Banyan threw off the blankets. Out stabbed his left hand to catch and tug at Throck's nearer ankle. At the same moment the right hand came into view holding a cocked Remington.

Jerked off balance by the unexpected attack, Throck staggered and his forefinger tightened involuntarily on the rifle's trigger. Winchester and Remington spoke at the same instant, the reports merging into one. Agony ripped into Banyan as he felt the impact of the bullet. Ranging upward, his own lead caught Throck under the chin to burst out of the top of the head, throwing the derby hat into the air. Then everything seemed to start happening at once.

At the sound of the shots, Nabbes and the Keebles brothers could not help looking to see what was happening. Wavering aside just as the trigger reached its rearmost point, Bud's revolver barked.

Even then it might have struck its target, but Derringer took advantage of the diversion and flung himself aside.

Going down in a rolling dive, Derringer caught hold of Calamity's Colt in passing. His fingers closed on the hand-fitting curves of the butt. With a heave, he pitched the belt away and the holster slid smoothly from the gun. As he landed, Derringer started to fan the Colt's hammer. Three shots slashed upward, driving into Bud's chest as the youngster tried to return his revolver to its target. Maybe the Navy Colt lacked its big Army brother's shock power, but three bullets from it carried more than enough impact to do their work. Spinning backward, Bud lost hold of his gun and measured his length on the ground.

Attention brought back by the commotion, Fenn saw his brother go down. With a snarl of rage, he began to swivel the rifle around toward the gambler. By the fire Banyan fought down the pain which tore through him as he saw Derringer's peril. With an effort, he lined the Remington and squeezed its trigger. Lead slammed into Fenn's ribs, deflecting his rifle just a shade as it cracked. Derringer felt a seering sensation as if somebody had raked his left thigh with a hot iron. However, he swung the Colt and thumbed a bullet into Fenn's chest, seeing the man collapse and let the rifle slide from limp hands.

Letting out a hiss of fury, Nabbes snaked his hand under his jacket and brought out his Remington Double Derringer. At which point Calamity also took a part in the affair. Although Derringer held her Colt, the girl did not count herself unarmed or helpless. In fact, she carried on her person a weapon just as deadly and efficient in its way as a revolver. Flashing across, Calamity's fingers closed on the handle of her whip and slipped it free. With the lash lying partially extended behind her, she did not need to waste a single motion. Around and forward curled the length of carefully plaited leather, whistling through the air like a living, thinking thing.

Even as Nabbes brought out the hide-out gun, he felt something wrap around his wrist with crushing, agonizing force. While slightly lighter, although not shorter, than the average male freight-driver's whip, Calamity's packed plenty of power. A cry of pain broke from Nabbes as the wrist-bones snapped. Nor did Calamity allow the impact alone to incapacitate the little man. Tugging back on the handle, she increased the agony to the injured arm. The Derringer fell from useless fingers at the pull.

Broken wrist or not, Nabbes attempted to continue the fight. Still held by the whip's lash, he dropped to his knees and tried to reach the gun with his left hand.

"Leave it!" Derringer yelled, turning the Navy Colt in the little man's direction after helping to drop Fenn.

The order proved needless. Once again Calamity gave a savage jerk at the handle of her whip and fresh pain caused Nabbes to forget his intention. Shaking free the lash, Calamity brought it snaking back ready to strike again. Under the combined threat of whip and Colt, Nabbes knew better than continue his attempt.

"Are you hit bad, Derry?" asked the girl, seeing blood on his leg.

"I'll do. But Sultan's caught it hard," the gambler replied. "You'd best see to him. I can handle Nabbes."

Looking around quickly, Calamity saw that only the little man of the gang needed supervision. Then she turned and headed to where Banyan was sitting, a hand clasped to the right sight of his chest. Even as she looked, the Remington slipped out of Banyan's hand. Leaving Derringer to watch Nabbes, she darted forward.

Hooves thundered and a man tore into sight

astride a fast-running horse. Noting his town-style clothing, Calamity bent and scooped up Banyan's Remington. She did not know who the newcomer might be, but aimed to take no chances.

"Boss!" the man yelled, bringing his horse to a rump-scraping halt and leaping from its saddle at Banyan's side. "Boss, how bad is it?"

"Lemme get to him!" Calamity ordered.

"Who're y——?" began the man, turning an angry, protective face to her.

"Sh-She's all right, Turk," Banyan croaked. "S-. . . Saved m-my life yes'day."

Instantly the newcomer's plain, somewhat stupid cast of features took on a different aspect. An expression of concern came as his eyes went to the blood which was spreading over the front of Banyan's shirt. Clearly Banyan's explanation satisfied him that Calamity could be trusted, for he raised no objections as the girl knelt at the big man's side.

"How bad is it?" Turk asked.

"Damned bad," admitted the girl frankly. "Can that hoss run?"

"Real good."

"Then get on it and head for town as fast as you can go. Bring a doctor out here soon's you can."

"Bu——"

"Do it, Turk," Banyan groaned.

"Sure, boss. Is she the ga——?"

"For Tophet's sake ride!" Calamity snapped.

Throwing another very worried look at Banyan, the man ran to his horse. He went into the saddle at a bound and set spurs to work. After watching the man head back in the direction from which he had come, Calamity turned to look at Banyan. Striking at close range, the bullet had torn straight through the big man's chest. Calamity knew that only a miracle might save him. Yet she wasted no time in idle thought.

"Lie down again," she ordered and dashed toward her wagon. In passing she saw Derringer sitting on the ground at Fenn's side, holding the man's rifle and watching Nabbes wade across the stream.

"I sent him on his way," the gambler gritted. "How's Sultan?"

"Hit bad. Can you hold out until after I've done what I can for him?"

"I reckon so. Give me something to cover the gash with and stop the bleeding, then I'll do."

Continuing on her way to the wagon, Calamity climbed inside. When travelling, she always carried cloth for bandages and a variety of herbal medicines the use of which she had learned from an old

Pawnee woman who worked for Killem. Gathering all she would need, she returned to Derringer. A low groan from Banyan prevented her from doing more than hand a length of white cloth to the gambler before hurrying to the big man's side.

After a short time Calamity returned to Derringer's side. He noticed the pallor under her tan and strain showing on her face. Blood stained her hands, showing that she had been attending to Banyan's wound.

"I'll do what I can for you now, Derry," she said. "Sultan's unconscious. I hope he stays that way."

"Yeah," Derringer agreed.

"Reckon Nabbes'll be back?" the girl asked, sinking to a knee at his side.

"Nope. He's had a bellyfull."

"How'd they find us?" Calamity said, reaching to the cloth on the wound.

"Luck, guess-work, could be either," Derringer answered, realizing that she was talking in an effort to stay calm for the work ahead. "I'd say one of them was ahead of the others and saw us camped here. Only they figured they couldn't come up in the night without enough noise to wake us. So they waited for daylight and moved in."

While only guessing to help Calamity, Derringer had unwittingly hit on the truth. After leaving Tribune, the gang had made slow progress due to being unable to hire good horses. For the rest, it had happened much as the gambler suggested.

When she exposed the wound, Calamity let out a low gasp. Running from just above the knee, a bloody furrow laid open the flesh to the top of the hip. Blood still ran sluggishly and Calamity guessed Derringer must be in agony.

"I'm going to have to spoil these fancy pants, Derry," she said, deftly slitting along the seam with a knife. "Nope, this's no use either. The pants'll have to come off."

"Here?"

"You figuring on walking into town first?"

"No, but——" Derringer spluttered, then he tried to rise. "I'll ta——"

"Here," Calamity said, reaching for his waist-belt. "Let me do it."

"You—— But—— You're a——"

Ignoring the gambler's incoherent gaspings, Calamity unfastened the belt and unbuttoned the fly. Then she carefully worked off Derringer's trousers and underpants, tossing them aside.

"Can't see's you've anything to be ashamed of," she commented. "What I'm going to do, I'll likely hurt a mite, Derry. Got some bark from a pepper-wood tree here. Chew on it to ease the pain."

"You're quite a gal, Calamity Jane," Derringer breathed, accepting the piece of bark she held out.

"I've never doubted *that*," she answered, with just a touch of the old Calamity back in her voice. "Get to chewing. I'll cover the nick with powdered witch-hazel leaves to slow the bleeding while I get some other stuff. If there's a balsam fir, white pine or slippery elm across the creek. I'll do a better job of fixing.

Before crossing the stream, Calamity built up the fire which Banyan had kept going all night. She set water to heat in a pan and coffee-pot, then headed into the woods where she found a slippery elm tree. Gathering some of its bark, twigs and young leaves, she returned to the camp. Without wasting time, she set to work mashing her gatherings into the water that bubbled in the pan. Behind her, Banyan moved restlessly and she heard him speak. Turning, she saw his eyes remained closed and guessed that delirium caused the words.

"They're dead at last," Banyan muttered. "Now I can get ri—— Damn it, there's no pretty French nester gal at Tor Hill."

Although the words reached Calamity's ears, they barely registered on her conscious mind. At that moment she found herself with too much on hand to think about what she heard. While waiting for the mess in the pan to boil, she returned and looked at Derringer's wound. The powdered witch-hazel leaves spread into the furrow had dried up the flow of blood, but she knew it would start to run again when he moved.

"We'll still have to chance it," she told the gambler. "Lean on me, get up and then try to keep your leg still.

At the cost of some pain, Derringer obeyed the girl. Fortunately Calamity led a life which kept her strong and healthy. For all that, sweat soaked her by the time she had supported the gambler and helped him across to the fire. Lowering Derringer to the ground, she looked anxiously at his wound. Blood was trickling from the center of the furrow, but not much and the last of the powder from Calamity's box went on the place to stem the flow.

Working as fast as possible, Calamity made the boiled slippery-elm shreds into a poultice. All the time Banyan continued to talk incoherently, but nothing he said made any sense that Derringer could understand. Or did it?

"Damn it, Ed. There's no gal at Tor Hill!" Banyan muttered. "If I thought you'd sent me—— Can't sell the damned things while they're alive——"

So it went on, vague words, meaningless apparently; about the War, the saloon business, the town, the trip he hoped to make to Europe. Mingled among it all he referred to various women, debating which of them he should take on the trip, if any.

"Smart gal, Rachel, she'd know her way around," the big man muttered. "Only she'd want to see operas and all them high-toned do-dads. Won't Velma make 'em open their eyes. What a gal, what a build. She'd have fellers round her like flies on a honey-pot like always—and I'd wind up knocking some of 'em all ways. Don't go for that in Europe. Joan, good old Joan. I never fed better'n when you cooked it, Joan gal. Can't see you in Paris, France though, Joan gal. Maybe if I got Sal in skirts instead of them pants—— Naw, she'd never do—"

"Poor bastard," Calamity breathed, darting a glance at Banyan as she brought the poultice to Derringer. "This's going to hurt a mite, Derry. But it'll draw out any poison."

A gasp of pain broke from Derringer as the heat bit into his wound. Gently Calamity wrapped a bandage around the poultice, fixing it into place. At any other time Derringer might have felt embarrassed, but the girl handled him with all the chilling impartiality of a trained nurse.

"Whooee!" he breathed when she finished. "That stings."

"Likely," she replied. "Now let's see if we can get your pants on. I don't know how long it'll be afore the doctor gets here. But happen he finds you like this, it could plumb ruin my good name."

"Small chance of that, damnit!" Derringer snorted, knowing the girl was speaking to take his—and her—mind off their troubles. "Here's me all undressed and r'aring to go——"

"And that leg stops you going any place," Calamity pointed out. "Come on, let's get your pants on."

With that task done, Calamity continued working. She made coffee, then attended to the horses. A call from Derringer brought her across to the fire.

"It's Sultan," he said.

The big man's eyes were open and he was trying to raise himself up, weakly gesturing to his feet.

"M-My boots——!" he croaked.

"I'll take 'em off," Calamity promised, knowing that many men dreaded the thought of dying with their boots on.

"Gi-Give 'em—Doc Fir—— He—knows what to do—with—'em."

Feeling puzzled Calamity tried to ease off the boots without hurting their wearer. Blood ran down Banyan's chin, trickling out of his mouth.

Setting the foot down, she sprang to kneel at his side. From all signs she knew the end must be near. Rising, she scanned the range toward the distant town but saw no sign of human movement. A shudder ran through the big frame, then Banyan lay still. Calamity sat at his side, knowing that only the arrival of the doctor—and a miracle after that—could save Banyan.

"You've done everything you can, Calam," Derringer said gently, laying a hand on her sleeve.

"C-Calam!" Banyan spoke weakly. "I-I'm near done, aren't I?"

"N-No," lied the girl. "You'll be up chasi——"

"Angels maybe," he interrupted. "Li-Listen, gal. I'm getting weak and mightn't finish or be able to repeat it——"

"Yes?"

"The Russians' jewellery's hid in my well."

Chapter 8

AFTER MAKING HIS REMARKABLE STATEMENT ABOUT the jewellery, Banyan sank back into unconsciousness. Although he rambled on about various things, he made no further reference to the matter. Calamity remained at the big man's side, waiting to do anything that might ease him. Then, as Turk came into sight accompanied by two more men, Banyan shuddered. Blood gushed from the man's mouth, his powerful frame quivered and went limp.

"No!" Calamity gasped, yet she knew the end had come and skilled medical assistance had arrived too late. "Oh Lord, no!"

"Easy, gal!" Derringer said, laying a gentle hand on her arm. "You did all you could."

"He's still dead," the girl groaned. "And with them so close."

"Listen, Calam!" Derringer said urgently. "There's not much time. The sheriff's going to ask questions. Tell him everything, except about the jewellery."

"Why not that?"

"We know somebody aimed to have him killed and, seeing's how he saved my life, I want to get whoever it is."

"And me!" Calamity stated grimly.

"It could be over those jewels," Derringer said. "Way I heard it, they're worth plenty. So we say nothing and wait. Maybe somebody'll start asking questions about them. And if somebody does, we've got us a suspect, gal."

"What'll we do then?"

"We'll likely think of something. There's another thing to think on. We've no way to know who we can trust. Whoever tried to have Sultan killed, if he did it for the jewels, won't take kind to us knowing about 'em. We might easy be next."

"So let's tell and see what happens!" Calamity hissed, watching the men approaching on tired, hard-pushed horses.

"Sure we will, hot-head," the gambler agreed. "Only not until after we know the lie of the land.

And don't forget that Sultan might've been wandering in his mind——"

"He didn't look it," Calamity protested.

"But he could still have been. Let folks get word about it and every money-hungry son-of-a-bitch in the Territory'll be moving in looking for it."

"You're starting to sound like Cap'n Fog," the girl smiled, seeing the wisdom of the other's words.

"I should be half as smart," Derringer answered seriously. "Now don't you forget. Tell everything straight, except for what Sultan said about the jewels."

If anyone had been asked to guess the identities of the men who rode with Turk, a mistake would be excusable. Dressed in jeans, a tan shirt and Stetson hat, a Freeman Army revolver hanging holstered at his side, Doctor Eben Fir was as lean as a buffalo-wolf after a hard winter, with a face tanned to the color of old saddle leather by exposure to the elements. He rode with relaxed, competent ease; hardly surprising considering that he had served many years as a surgeon in the U.S. Cavalry and made many of his house calls on the back of a horse.

Fat as a butter-ball, Sheriff Oscar Wendley gave the impression of town-dwelling ease and presented an air of lassitude. He wore a neat town suit, but the stiff collar of the shirt looked somewhat too large and did not close tightly about the throat in the prevailing fashion. Taken against his general neatness, the collar appeared almost untidy. Yet it served a useful purpose in allowing him to turn his head from side to side unhindered. Instead of carrying his ivory-handled Army Colt in a holster, he had thrust it butt forward in the silk sash about his waist.

Despite his appearance, the sheriff did not act in a lethargic manner on arrival. After the doctor announced Banyan's death, Wendley prowled around the camp. He examined the bodies and weapons that lay around, and went over the ground in a way which showed he knew at least the rudiments of reading sign. Then he returned and, while Fir attended to Derringer's wound, asked to be told what had happened. From questions he asked at various points in Calamity's narrative, she realized that Wendley could read sign with some skill. Nor was he made of flabby fat. Hard, firm flesh formed that well-padded body and she bet he could move fast when the situation demanded it.

Beginning with how she and Banyan met, the girl told the full story apart from his reference to the Russians' jewellery. A faint scowl came to Wendley's face as she told how they decided murder rather than robbery had been the motive of the attack. Then she continued, explaining how Nabbes' gang had arrived and describing the way in which Banyan had acted.

"That'd be just like Sultan," Wendley said, nodding his head. "That one who run, was he hurt?"

"I'd say my whip bust his wrist," Calamity replied. "Only with Sultan and Derry both shot, I'd too much on my hands to want him around needing watching."

"I'll take after him, Sheriff!" Turk snarled.

"We'll both go after him when we're through here," Wendley answered. "Mind if I talk to the gent without you on hand, Miss Calamity?"

At any other time the suggestion that she might be lying would have aroused Calamity to anger. However, she knew that Wendley was merely performing his duty. Any capable peace officer would take the same precaution when investigating a multiple killing. So she withdrew and started to gather up her belongings ready to continue her journey. Sultan Banyan lay dead, but the rest of life must go on. In her wagon were supplies that must be delivered to the town.

"Are you feeling all right, Calamity?" Doctor Fir inquired, coming up as she placed the blankets Derringer had used in the wagon.

"Sure," she replied.

"You did well, gal. Without your help, Sultan'd've died sooner and in bad pain. Derringer there should thank you, too. You did a good job patching up that leg."

"Thanks for saying so, Doc. Hey though, Sultan told me to give you his boots. Allowed you'd know what to do with them."

"Hell, yes!" Fir grunted. "I'd forgotten about that. Lord! This's a blow. I wonder what brought old Sultan out here?"

"He didn't say," Calamity replied, forgetting the garbled references Banyan had made to the nester girl at Tor Hill. In the West one did not question a chance acquaintance's motives for travelling, so her lack of knowledge could be excused.

At the same moment Wendley was posing an identical question to Derringer. However, the answer came from Turk, not the gambler.

"The boss heard there was a real pretty lil French gal living out by Tor Hill. So he told me he'd be headed that way to see her."

"That'd be Sultan's way," the sheriff admitted.

"When he didn't get back by midnight, I figured I'd best come out looking for him," Turk went on. "Damn it. Why didn't I start out sooner?"

"Did Sultan expect trouble?" Derringer asked.

"Naw!" snorted Turk. "I just watch out for him is all."

With that the young man turned and slouched away. After watching him go, the sheriff returned his attention to Derringer.

"Sultan say something to you that made you think he did expect trouble?"

"Nope," admitted the gambler. "Only if we called it right, somebody hired those three jaspers to kill him. That spells trouble to me."

"Can't think who it'd be," Wendley said. "Sultan'd a way of getting on real well with folks. Anybody'd lost in his place could get five to ten bucks broke money for the asking. He treated everybody, help, customers, other saloon-keepers decent enough."

"How about his wives? He mentioned something about four of 'em. Was he joking?"

"He'd had one wife as I know on, no more," Wendley replied. "I've heard him talk about the others and allus figured it to be a joke. He sure was one for the gals, old Sultan."

"You'll be staying in Banyan for a spell?" the sheriff asked, after a few more questions about the affair.

"As long as you need me around," Derringer promised. "I planned to stay on for a spell, anyways."

At that moment the doctor walked up and said, "If you're done, Oscar, I'd like to get Derringer here to town so I can look to his leg properly."

"Sure, Eb," the sheriff answered. "When you get back, tell Tyler Kitson to come out with the hearse for Sultan."

"He'll need more than the hearse with three here and three back on the trail," Fir commented. "I'd best have him bring a wagon as well."

"Sure. It can load these three, then follow Turk and me to the others."

"One thing," Derringer said, looking at the sheriff. "Can you find out who told Sultan about the gal at Tor Hill?"

"Why?" asked the doctor.

"Those gun-hands were waiting on the trail for him to come back and there was no gal out at Tor Hill."

"How'd you know that?" Wendley demanded suspiciously.

"He said something about it while he was rambling in his mind," Derringer replied. "I didn't think much on it at the time, the rest he said wasn't making much sense."

"So you reckon somebody told Sultan about the gal, knowing that he'd be hide-bound sure to go take a look," Wendley said. "Fixing to have him killed on the way back to town."

"That's how it looks to me," Derringer agreed. "Maybe Turk'd know."

"I'll ask him," the sheriff said. "Only not now. He'd not discuss Sultan's business in front of the doc here even. He's coming with me. I don't want him taking off after that feller got away on his own. Reckon when we're alone I can learn all I need from him."

"Oscar's calling it right, Derringer," Fir went on. "Turk was real loyal to Sultan. Lord. I'd hate to be the man who tried to have him killed should Turk learn his name."

"And me," grunted Wendley. "Like to see you when I get back to town, Mr. Derringer."

"Sure enough, Sheriff," the gambler promised, and the doctor helped him to the side of Calamity's wagon.

During the journey to town, Derringer tried to learn more about the situation from Fir. Although willing to discuss Banyan's known past, the doctor proved reticent on the matters which interested Calamity and the gambler most. Not wishing to arouse Fir's suspicions, Derringer refrained from pressing too hard for information. Calamity followed the gambler's lead and soon Fir sank into silence. Nor, with him riding alongside the wagon, could Derringer and the girl compare views on the dead man's last conscious statement.

The town of Banyan proved bigger than Derringer expected, with the log-walled fort in the distance to the west. Turk Street split the town into two almost equal sections. Along its length could be found most of the business premises, saloons and other places of entertainment, a large hotel, the civic offices neatly compressed into one building. Further testifying to the town's size and importance, Wells Fargo maintained a large depot and stage-coaches branched out from it to nearly every point of the compass. One of the gaily painted coaches rolled by the fort on its way into town even as Calamity's wagon went by the hotel.

"It's as good as the Granada in Tribune," the doctor commented, nodding to the latter establishment in passing. "My office's along the street there, Calamity. Between the jail and that store."

"Want for me to take you down there?" she asked.

"I reckon we can manage," Fir assured her. "You'll find Sam Werner's store opposite the Harem."

"Need me to collect you when the doc's finished, Derry?"

"Can I walk, Doc?" Derringer inquired.

"I'm not fixing to put in any stitches," Fir replied. "So if you keep it clean, dry, stop out of any fist-fights or foot-races, it ought to be all right. You've got that cane to take the weight."

"Then I'll walk back to the hotel when I'm through, Calam," Derringer told the girl. "I'll book a room there for you, unless you've other ideas."

"There'll do," grinned Calamity, halting the wagon and dropping to the ground to help the gambler dismount.

After closer examination and application of clean bandages, the doctor helped Derringer to don the trousers belonging to the town suit. He found that he could walk slowly, yet well enough and with little discomfort, provided he used the cane-gun for its former purpose. In a way the wound might prove advantageous as it allowed him to carry the cane without arousing suspicion. Paying for his treatment, he left the office and made his way back toward the hotel.

Along the street, the stage-coach had arrived and disgorged its passengers. One of them, followed by a couple of the loungers who hung around the depot carrying a trunk, was approaching the hotel's main entrance. Studying the passenger, Derringer concluded that he had never seen such a sultry, sensual woman. Despite having just completed a stage-coach journey, she had contrived to keep her piled-up blonde hair almost faultlessly in place under the tiny, impractical hat. Nor did her beautiful features show signs of the journey. The pert little nose and full, pouting lips added to the attraction of the langorous, come-to-bed eyes. Under the travelling dress of daring cut lay an almost perfect hour-glass figure, rich full bosom exposed to the limits of modesty by the decollete of the neck.

Burdened only by a tiny parasol in her left hand and vanity bag hanging from the right, she slunk along the sidewalk with a hip-swinging, sensuous grace that drew male eyes and scowls of feminine disapproval from the other pedestrians. The two loafers carrying her trunk remained behind her and never took their eyes from the way the bustle moved under the dress.

Taking in the girl's appearance and mannerisms, Derringer first thought she might be a saloon worker. Then he noted the costly material of the dress and that the jewellery she wore seemed to be both genuine and expensive. No saloon worker, unless she be the boss' favorite. A stage performer, maybe, on her way to appear at the theater? The lack of baggage seemed to rule out that possibility. Not a successful prostitute either; such a person would not be allowed to enter the Plaza Hotel. Still wondering who she might be, Derringer followed her into the hotel's lobby.

The fittings and state of cleanliness inside compared favorably with that of the Granada in Tribune, Derringer decided as he looked around. Behind the desk, the clerk stared at the blonde, grabbed up his pen and poked it toward the neck of the ink-pot.

Only two of the hotel's residents were in the lobby, both women who eyed the newly arrived blonde with disapproval but no sign of recognition. Seated by the door, the tall rusty-haired woman reminded Derringer of all the schoolmarms he had ever known. In her late thirties at least, she might have been beautiful but for the chilling, stand-no-nonsense aspect of her face. Under the severe black of an expensive town suit lay a figure that, given chance, might come close to the blonde's in richness of curves.

Just entering the lobby from the dining room, the other woman seemed out of place in such surroundings. While her buxom figure was clad in good, costly clothing, she gave the impression that such had not always been the case. Wives of newly rich businessmen, or up-from-the-ranks army officers often looked that way. Not bad looking, although nothing compared with the blonde, she had a good, sturdy shape.

Undulating her way across to the desk, the blonde halted and favored the clerk with a winning smile.

"I'm Mrs. Banyan," she said. "And I'm sure my husband would want me to have the best room in the house."

Shock twisted at the clerk's beaming features and he stabbed the pen down hard into the inkpot.

"M-Mrs. Banyan?" he repeated in a high-pitched, squeaky voice.

"Yes?" said two voices.

The other two women spoke, each sounding as if she were answering her name. Then both of them converged on the desk where the clerk stared open-mouthed from one to another of them. Slowly realization came to the three women and each looked at the other two with some surprise showing on her face. If offered a bet on the matter, Derringer would have put his money on the one with rusty hair recovering first.

She did. Stiffening slightly, she spoke in a well-educated-sounding voice.

"You ladies must be related to my husband."

"I never knew Sultan had any brothers, or other kin," the blonde answered.

"Su——!" gasped the one with black hair. "Bu–But I'm married to Wallace."

"I never called him either Claude or Wallace," the blonde stated. "But he's my husband—and I've never divorced him."

"Neither did I!" bristled the black-haired woman, her accent working-class Kansan.

"And I can assure you both that I am also Claude Wallace Banyan's wife," the rusty-haired woman put in. "It seems that we are all married to the same man and that two of us can have no legal standing."

"I married Sultan in December sixty-five!" the blonde announced and reached toward the mouth of the vanity bag. "And I've got my marriage lines to prove it."

"But he married me in June sixty-nine," the black-haired woman said, showing more concern over the situation than the other two. "And I've got proof with me."

"My marriage, which is still legally binding, was

in December, sixty-one, ladies," the rusty-haired woman declared. "Which I can also prove. So I——" At which point she became aware that three men stood listening to every word spoken. "This is not a matter we can discuss before these people. May I suggest that we go up to my room and continue our business in private?"

"It would be best," agreed the black-haired Mrs. Banyan.

"Sure," the blonde went on. "Leave my trunk by the desk, boys, and thanks."

Although the loafers would normally have expected a tip for their services, the scene they had witnessed drove all such thoughts from their heads. So they just stood gaping as the three women walked up the stairs. From what Derringer could hear, introductions were being made.

"My name is Rachel B——" the rusty-haired one said, then chopped off the last word as being superfluous under the circumstances.

"I'm Velma," the blonde replied.

"M-My name's Joan," the third wife went on. Of the three, she sounded the most shocked at finding her husband had two more wives. "B-But I can't believe——"

"Nor me," Velma replied, darting a glance at the

other two as if trying to see what her husband found in them after being with her.

"I hope that neither of you ladies has any children," Rachel remarked as they reached the head of the stairs. "I have none——"

"Well, I'll be——!" gasped the clerk as the women's voices died away. Then he stared down at the register, tapping the top line of the newly started page. "So that's how I missed the other two. One of 'em come in last night and signed over the page, while I was at home. The other come in on the morning stage." With his curiosity partially satisfied, he looked at Derringer and went on, "Don't that beat all. Do you reckon it's right about them all being married to ole Sultan?"

"I don't know," Derringer replied. "And I'm not fixing to ask. Right or wrong, I don't reckon Sultan or Turk'd go much on having word of it spread around town about this——"

"Especially Turk," the clerk interrupted, worry on his face.

"Like you say, especially Turk," Derringer agreed and glared at the other three men. "Now I'm not fixing to say a word. So if it does leak out, there'll only be *three* who could have started it. *Savvy?*"

From the expressions on their faces, the trio savvied. Clearly Turk carried some weight around Banyan; enough to ensure the trio's silence until the sheriff returned. So Derringer gave his attention to booking rooms for Calamity and himself and wondering what would be the next fantastic development in Sultan Banyan's affairs.

Chapter 9

CALAMITY JANE MIGHT BE A TOUCH HOT-HEADED, a mite tactless and somewhat reckless at times, but she could be relied upon to keep her eyes open and take notice of anything interesting she saw. After the incidents of the past few days, she still could not relax, even though approaching her final delivery point. Her eyes continued to dart glances around, studying the people she passed and the lay-out of the town.

Standing at the end of the Big Herd Saloon's strip of sidewalk, a medium-sized man, wearing glasses with thick lens, watched the wagon go by. By the saloon's main entrance stood a tall, lean gambler, swarthily handsome with an air of toughness apparent to a student of western human nature. Lounging with a shoulder against the wall, he kept his right hand thumb-hooked into the gunbelt close to the Adams Army revolver in the fast-draw holster. He too studied the wagon with some interest. Enough to attract Calamity's attention under the circumstances. Of course the sight of a pretty gal dressed in such a manner and handling the ribbons of a six-horse team could be counted on to draw male eyes. Yet Calamity felt that more than that was causing the two men to watch her approach.

Although the pair had nothing in common, the one a saloon worker or professional gambler and the other apparently a member of the lower middle-class workers—a bank clerk maybe, or a senior employee in a store—Calamity's instincts told her they shared a mutual interest. Something in the way they stood, each exhibiting just too casual a disregard for the other's presence, reminded the girl of peace officers keeping watch on suspected premises—or outlaws studying the scene of their next crime. Yet the latter seemed unlikely for the bank lay back along the street and, successful though it might be, Sam Werner's store was an unlikely prospect for a robbery.

In some way the two men seemed vaguely familiar to Calamity. She tried to place them, but could not. This being her first visit to Banyan, she had not met them in the town. Of course she travelled around and saw a whole heap of people. Maybe the two had been in some other place. Or it could be that she was making a mistake in thinking she recognized them.

Putting aside her thoughts on the men, Calamity brought the wagon to a halt before Werner's general store. She booted on the brake, then swung to the sidewalk as the store's door opened. Coming out, the stocky, cheerful-looking owner showed his surprise at finding a girl instead of the usual male driver.

"You're from Dobe Killem?" Werner asked.

"Sure. None of the other drivers'd come in and he allowed you'd likely need the gear in the wagon."

"I do. This's the first time you've been here, Calamity."

"Sure, and it's been some trip," she answered, not surprised that the store-keeper had identified her. All Killem's regular customers knew she drove for him. "I'm sorry I couldn't get a deer for you on the way in."

"Country's getting all hunted out down that ways," Werner said. "I'll have my boys come out and unload."

"Here's the bill-of-lading," Calamity told him, producing the sheet of paper and pleased that she had found a suitable excuse for her lack of hunting success without her needing to go into details. "Check it off, will you. Say, who's the tinhorn across the street?"

"Him? That's Ted Claggert, floor-boss over to the Big Herd."

"Been around town for long?"

"Came in with Edgar Turnbull and worked here ever since. That's maybe eighteen months. Why?"

"He looked kind of familiar," Calamity answered. "But if he's been around town for that long, I don't reckon he is. How about that dude along there?"

"Can't say I've ever seen him afore," Werner answered, after a casual look along the street in the man's direction but without actually gazing straight at him. "What's up, Calam?"

"I'm just a mite uneasy," she replied. "Let's get the unloading done so's I can see to my team."

That was always the freighter's code; care for the load and team first, with personal needs coming a long way second. So the girl supervised the unloading by Werner's two sons. Boxes, barrels, sacks came off the wagon to be carried into the store; each item being ticked off the list Werner held. Due to the trouble at the last camp Calamity made a later start than she expected and the sun was sinking toward the western horizon before the work was completed.

"I done snuck off with a couple of boxes of gold 'n' jewels," she told Werner with a grin.

"So who needs them?" he answered. "The rest's here."

Before any more could be said, the door opened and Claggert entered. "Did those cards come in, Sam?" he asked.

"Right here," the store-keeper replied, indicating the box.

"Can I have twenty decks? I tell you, we need 'em across at the Big Herd. The ones we're using now're so thick that we have to pound 'em into the dealing boxes."

"I"ll see to it after I've dealt with Calamity here."

"Give the gent his cards, Sam," Calamity suggested. "I can wait."

A puzzled frown came and went across Werner's face like a flash. From all he had heard, Calamity Jane let nothing stand in the way of caring for her team. Then he remembered the interest she had shown in Claggert and realized that she wanted to see the sale completed. Wondering what caused her interest, he set about opening the box.

The same thought came to Calamity as she moved in a casual-seeming manner to stand by the window. If questioned, she would have been hard put to supply a satisfactory answer. Yet something about the floor-manager's attitude, although he did no more than stand across the street, had struck her as suspicious. That, and the fact that she felt sure she knew Claggert, caused Calamity to delay attending to her team. Looking across the street, she saw the dude still standing on the sidewalk and gazing with intent expectancy toward the store.

"There's something cock-eyed somewheres," she mused. "Only I'm damned if I know where."

Not in the instant purchase of the cards. Any saloon or gambling house would wish to keep a supply of new decks, for old cards picked up marks on their backs by which a smart player might gain information. Nor would Werner, as jobber for Bletchley & Sons, keep the arrival of fresh stock a secret. For all that, Calamity's every instinct told her something was wrong.

With the purchase completed, Claggert left the store. Calamity saw him cross the sidewalk and head toward the Big Herd, then swung her eyes in the direction of the other man. Giving a slight inclination of his head, in reply to a nod from Claggert, the dude turned and walked off along the alley of the saloon.

"Is something wrong, Calam?" Werner asked.

"Nope," she replied. "Like I said, I'm just a mite uneasy. It's been some trip. I'll go see to the team."

"Put the wagon around back and the horses in my stable, if you like," the store-keeper suggested.

"Thanks," she said. "I'll do just that."

Accompanied by Werner's two sons, Calamity took the wagon to the rear of the building. After unhitching and attending to her team, she gathered her warbag, Derringer's grip and the carbine from the wagon. Watched by the admiring youngsters, she walked off toward the hotel.

Still in something of a daze at the thought of what he learned from the three women, the desk clerk hardly raised an eyebrow when Calamity told him that she had come for Miss Canary's reservation. At another time he might have raised objections to the girl's appearance, but that evening did no more than hand her a key and tell a bell-boy to show her to her room.

On reaching the first floor, with the bags carried by a much-impressed youngster, Calamity saw a second bell-boy standing at one of the doors talking with a stern-faced woman. When the words reached her ears, all Calamity's skill as a poker player went into preventing showing her surprise.

"Ole Sul—Mr. Banyan ain't down to the Harem, ma'am," the bell-boy was saying. "And they don't know when he'll be back."

"Then go back and tell them that Mrs. Banyan says to send here with word the moment he returns," the woman replied.

"Yes'm!" answered the boy, and scuttled away.

Calamity could hardly wait to put her warbag and carbine into her room. Yet she forced herself to act as if the brief conversation meant nothing to her. Putting her property on the bed, she tipped the boy and waited until he left. Then she took Derringer's bag to his room and knocked on the door.

"How's the leg?" she asked, walking in when he opened up.

"It's still there," he replied, and she could tell that it hurt enough for him to be aware of it.

"You'll never guess who I've just seen across the hall," she said eagerly.

"Who?"

"Mrs. Banyan!"

For a dramatic announcement, the words received little success. Not that she expected Derringer to dance around the room, but felt that he ought to at least act a mite surprised. Instead he merely said, "Which one?"

"Huh?" Calamity grunted.

"There's three of 'em in the hotel," the gambler explained. "At least, they all claim to be Mrs. Banyan."

"*Three!*" Calamity yelped.

"Three," Derringer agreed. "And you sure'd make a swell poker player, way you keep calm."

"Calm be damned! It's not the son-of-a-bitching kind of news a gal expects to hear. Three of 'em, you say. Whooee! Wonder where the fourth 'n' is?"

"She'll most likely turn up comes supper-time. Thing being, what brings 'em all here—today."

"Hell, yes!" breathed Calamity. "They got here the day he died."

"The day *after* he was supposed to die," Derringer corrected.

"Did they know each other?"

"Not as I could see, and I watched real careful."

"Being married to two-three other gal's not what I'd expect a feller to tell his wife," Calamity said in a wondering voice. "Whooee! Wasn't that Sultan some hairy-chested he-coon. Hey, though! Except among Mormons and such, having more'n one wife at a time's agin the law, ain't it?"

"Sure is," agreed Derringer. "Thing is, what do we do now?"

"Huh?"

"Do we go in and tell 'em to see what happens? Or shall we leave that to the sheriff?"

A knock at the door took the decision from their hands. On opening it, Derringer found Doctor Fir—now clad in a sober black suit—and another man standing outside. Big, heavy-framed, with an air of pompous arrogance on a granite-hard face, the man wore expensive clothing of excellent town cut, if slightly out of fashion, and did not appear to be armed.

"Derringer," Fir greeted. "This's Counsellor Edsteed Gilbert. He's acted for Sultan, so I figured he ought to know about this morning."

"Our business can't be discussed standing out here," Gilbert went on. "I have urgent need to see you and the young woman."

"He means Calamity," Fir said dryly, and Derringer could sense an undercurrent of antipathy between the two men, "Any idea where she might be, friend?"

"She's in here," Derringer answered. "Just now brought my bag up."

On entering the room, Gilbert studied Calamity with an air of mixed surprise and interest. However, he wasted no time before reaching into his jacket's inside pocket and removing a sheet of paper.

"Doctor Fir informed me of Sult—my client's death. A tragedy and a great loss to the community," he said. "It was my belief that he died intestate——"

"Nope," Calamity interrupted. "He got shot——"

"Intestate means he died without making a will, Calam," Derringer explained.

Giving a sniff, Gilbert continued, "Despite my assumption that he died intestate, a will has come to light."

"It was inside the lining of Sultan's right boot," Fir put in. "That's why he told you to give them to me."

"As I was saying," Gilbert said, throwing a baleful glare at the doctor. "A will has come to light. It is a somewhat unusual document and I felt that its contents should be communicated to you immediately."

"Us!" Calamity replied. "Why us? His wives're rooming across the hall."

"Wife?" Gilbert gasped.

"Sal—here?" Fir growled.

"Wives, not wife," Derringer corrected. "There's three of them."

"Thr——!" Fir began, while Gilbert stood open-mouthed and silent. "If this's a joke——"

"All you have to do is knock and ask," Derringer told him.

"Damn it, that's just what I'll do!" Fir shouted. "And if it is a——"

"Whether the ladies are, or are not, Sultan's wives is of no importance at the moment," Gilbert put in, rallying from his shock with an almost visible effort. Clearly the news that three women claiming to be his deceased client's wives hit him hard. However, he mastered his emotions and waved the sheet of paper. "This is a legally executed will and without a doubt genuine——"

"Thanks!" Fir snorted.

"You must admit that the terms are somewhat irregular, Doctor," Gilbert answered with pompous calm. "I mean this part here: 'And so, in view of the uncertainty of life, I leave my saloon to whoever is at my side when I die'! That clause alone might cause doubts as to the will's authenticity."

"Does that mean what I think it means?" Derringer inquired.

"It means, Mr. Derringer," Gilbert intoned solemnly, "that you and Miss Canary here are the owners of the Harem Saloon."

For a moment neither Calamity nor Derringer

spoke as they let the surprising news sink in. Then Calamity turned an amazed face to the gambler and she gasped, "Tell me I'm dreaming!"

"If you are, I'm having the same dream," he replied, and looked at Gilbert. "You mean that, just because we happened to be with Sultan when he died, we get to own the Harem?"

"Yes," agreed the lawyer. "With certain provisos. Such as keeping certain employees—there are ten of them—employed at an increased salary for a period of at least five years. Or, in the event that they wish to quit, paying them a lump sum equal to the said five years' salary. There is a sizeable bank balance as running expenses for the saloon, so you need not worry on the latter account."

Ever a good-hearted, generous girl, Calamity gave little thought to how the will affected her. Instead she pointed to the door and said, "But if those gals're Sultan's wives, they should have the place; not a couple of strangers, which's all me 'n' Derry are."

"The will was made of Sultan's own free will and desire," Gilbert replied. "Therefore it is legally binding. However, I think you need have no worries on the ladies' behalf. If they should be his wives, I feel certain that he will have made adequate provision for their future."

"Yeah, but——" Calamity began.

"As soon as Su—the body is brought into town and its personal effects released by the sheriff, we may know more about that," Gilbert interrupted. "I am instructed in the will to open his office safe, take out, read and act on the letter it contains."

"That's swell!" Calamity snorted. "Only there's three gals across the hall waiting for a husband who'll not be coming back."

"It would be best if the news was broken to them," Gilbert admitted. "I'll attend to it now."

"Maybe I'd best come along," Fir suggested. "Could be I'll be needed in my professional capacity."

"I'm coming!" Calamity stated flatly. "I want those gals to know I'm willing to hand 'em my share of the place. Hell, if I was partner in a saloon like the Harem, I'd be rich enough to marry and settle down—and I'd hate like hell for *that* to happen."

Derringer looked at Calamity with a gentle smile. All the stories folks told of her generosity appeared to be true; also about her sense of humor. However, he said nothing and let the others out of the room. One thing puzzled Derringer. Why did a lawyer like Gilbert calmly accept the news that three women each claimed to be his deceased client's wife?

Despite his air of arrogant pomposity, Gilbert proved himself remarkably tactful and adept at passing out bad news. After introducing himself as Banyan's lawyer, he gained access for the party to Rachel's room. The other two women sat inside, studying the newcomers with interest. Then Gilbert broke the news as gently as possible to them.

Watching the trio, Derringer read shock on each face. Yet none of them gave way to outbursts of grief. Clearly Rachel felt that the situation called for some explanation.

"You must excuse our lack of emotion," she said. "However, Claude was not what could be termed an ideal husband."

"I'd no complaints," purred Velma, but nobody took any notice of the comment.

"Did he leave a will?" Rachel demanded bluntly.

"A rather strange one," the lawyer admitted, then went into the details.

Still studying the women, Derringer could see nothing other than surprise on their faces as they listened to the contents of the will. He had hoped that one of them might reveal anger, or some such emotion, that might point to a motive for the attempt on Banyan's life. If any of the three had tried to have her husband killed in the hope of inheriting a prosperous business and considerable wealth, she hid it carefully.

"The will is valid?" Rachel asked.

"Perfectly, as far as I can see," Gilbert answered. "It was drawn up by a lawyer in Kansas City. Of course, it has yet to be probated."

"If I knew Sultan, and I reckon I did," Fir put in. "He'll not've left his wi—you wanting for anything."

"That's probably correct," Gilbert agreed soothingly. "Of course, we can't examine his personal documents until the sheriff returns."

"That is hardly the point!" Rachel snapped. "As Claude's wife, I feel that I have a better claim to his property than two strangers."

"I'm his wife too, you know!" Joan said grimly.

"And so am I!" Velma went on.

"I presume that each of you ladies can produce proof of your claims to being my client's wife?" asked Gilbert.

"I can!" all three replied at the same moment as hands dipped into vanity bags to produce their evidence.

"Of course two of the marriages are illegal," Rachel stated, with the confidence that came from knowing her own would not be one of them.

"I'm afraid that might not be true," Gilbert

told her, examining each woman's marriage certificate and returning it to her. "Can you remember who married you, Mrs. Banyan?—The priest, I mean?"

"It was one Claude found," Rachel, to whom the question had been directed, replied. "I would have preferred a more formal wedding, but we had to join a wagon-train headed west. So Claude brought a priest to perform the ceremony."

"I didn't pay much attention to the preacher," Velma answered in her turn. "Sultan found him and that was good enough for me."

"How about you, Mrs. Banyan?" asked Gilbert, looking at Joan.

"It was some preacher I had never seen before. I wanted the Reverend Hooper to officiate as I'd known him for years. He wasn't available and Wallace brought along this young deacon."

"And Su—my client never mentioned his religious beliefs to you?"

"Not to me," Velma replied. "We didn't waste time——"

"I fail to see what all this is leading up to, Counsellor!" Rachel interrupted. "As Claude and I were never divorced, the other two marriages can't be legal."

"I'm afraid you're wrong, Mrs. Banyan,"

Gilbert told her. "You see, my client was of the Mormon faith; which practices polygamy. If, as now seems probable, a Mormon priest performed the ceremonies, all three marriages *are* legal.

Chapter 10

"DERRY AND ME AREN'T IN FAVOR OF THIS NOTION," Calamity Jane told the group of people gathered in Banyan's private office on the first floor of the Harem Saloon. "If he aimed to give the place away, it should've come to you folk who've been with him from the start and helped to make it pay."

"If the boss'd've wanted it that way, he'd've said so," Ward Sharp, the floor-manager, replied. "We allus did what he said while he was here and we'll not go against his dying wishes."

A middle-sized man, Sharp made up his deficiencies in height with breadth and depth; and it was all hard flesh or solid muscle. Although wearing the dress-style of a professional gambler, his blunt-fingered hands looked more in keeping for a manual worker. From all the expression his face showed, hearing his boss had been murdered and willed the saloon to two complete strangers might be an everyday occurrence.

Behind the floor-manager stood four senior members of the staff. Goldie, the blonde, buxom, middle-aged but still good-looking boss girl; Buck Gitsen, supervisor of the gambling tables, tall, slim, elegant yet steel-spring tough; bald, stocky Harvey Cromer, the head bartender; big, burly, broken-nosed Sheb Cash, the top bouncer. None of them, not even Gitsen, kept such an impassive face as Sharp. All studied their new employers with calculating gaze, wondering what changes would be made. Goldie gave Calamity more attention than Derringer, sensing a possible threat to her position. As heads of their departments—although none of them regarded their work in such a manner—the quartet had been called upstairs to hear of the change of ownership and their increase in salary.

In view of the three wives' behavior, Calamity had lost her feelings of generosity and decided to let them sweat for a spell. So she made no mention of handing control of the saloon to them. Derringer followed her lead, wanting to see what developed.

After some argument, the wives had grudgingly accepted that Derringer and Calamity could claim to run the saloon until the will was probated. Fir helped their agreement by stating he believed the employees who mattered in the continued operation of the business—those present and the others mentioned as beneficiaries under the will—would insist on carrying out their late boss's instructions. Rather than see the saloon closed, the wives had given their consent to the arrangement. So Gilbert had brought Calamity and Derringer to the saloon to meet their staff.

"How'll the other folks take it?" Calamity asked, looking at Goldie.

"They'll do as they're told," the blonde answered, her face showing more grief than any of the wives had displayed over Banyan's death. "I suppose you'll be working the tables."

Which meant, as both she and Calamity knew, "Will you be taking my job?"

"Dressed like this?" grinned Calamity. "And I'd sure as hell not want to get into them fancy do-dads. Nope. I'm going to be a real boss, sit on my butt-end and watch the hired help do all the work."

If a touch weak due to grief, a corresponding grin came to Goldie's face. Calamity knew that she had gained a valuable friend. Probably she would have to prove herself to some of the girls, but she preferred not to be in conflict with the blonde. Unless Calamity missed her guess, Goldie knew how to take care of herself.

"I'll see they do it," Goldie promised.

"That's what you're here for," Calamity agreed. "Day I catch you driving my wagon, I'll take over here."

With harmony established between the distaff side, the men gave Derringer their attention. First Cash told Derringer of the bouncers' work.

"We don't get much trouble most times. Pay night's wild, but we can handle it. The Provost Marshal's boys help us with the soldiers. The boss didn't go for no worse rough-handling than necessary."

"I'll go along with that," Derringer answered.

"We've a good supply of liquor in," Cromer continued. "Enough to last us until the next shipment. It's stored down in the cellar if you'd like to take a look. Boss had us serve fair measure, good stuff and hand back the right change drunk or sober."

"You'll see it stays that way?" Derringer asked.

"That's what I get paid for."

"We run the usual games," Gitsen said. "Faro,

chuck-a-luck, black jack. There's a big poker game held down here that the boss played in every Saturday he could. You'll find everything the way you want it, Mr. Derringer."

Accepting the tribute to his honesty, Derringer nodded. "Great. And I don't go much on 'mistering.' The name's 'Frank.' "

While the men talked, Calamity looked around the office. Clearly Sultan Banyan had enjoyed his creature comforts. While the desk looked a plain, functional piece of equipment, the chairs offered more comfort and she could imagine the use to which he put the large, comfortable couch at the far side of the room. Paintings of women in various stages of undress decorated the walls and fancy vases stood about the room. Even the stoutly made safe looked decorative. So the two black objects standing on top of it struck Calamity as out of place in such opulent surroundings.

Curiosity aroused, Calamity walked over to the safe and picked up one of the objects. It had an oval-shaped body from which rose a wooden tail with cardboard fins, and stood on a flat metal base. Much to her surprise, she saw an open box of percussion caps by the wall at the rear of the safe. Then she heard Gilbert speak in a strained, frightened voice.

"D-Don't knock it, Miss Canary. That's a Ketchum hand-grenade."

Although she had never seen a hand-grenade, Calamity remembered hearing soldiers mention them. Of the various types experimented with during the War between the States, the Ketchum proved to be the most safe and reliable. Yet she could not imagine why Banyan had kept such potentially dangerous devices on his safe.

"Don't worry, Miss Calamity," Sharp grinned as she gingerly set down the grenade. "They're not primed."

"What in hell're they for?" she asked. "They sure ain't as fancy for looking at as them pictures."

"Figured they might come in handy if we ever got held up," the floor-manager explained. "This room looks down on the front of the place and there's allus somebody up there. Idea is that if we should be stuck up, anybody who can gets into the office, primes the bombs and tosses them down on the gang when they leave."

"That's not a bad notion," Derringer said.

"Boss used something like it in the War," Cash put in.

"You'd best show me how to prime the damned things, whatever that is," Calamity said.

"Not right now," Derringer objected. "Let's take a look around downstairs."

"Sure," Calamity agreed. "Say, where do you get the water you use in here from, a well?"

"No. Pump it up," Goldie replied. "Why?"

"I was figuring on taking a bath later," Calamity told her. "Come on, I've never seen a saloon 'cepting as a customer."

Leaving the office, Calamity and Derringer stood with the others and looked over their inheritance. The balcony on which they stood stretched around both sides and the rear, with rooms on two of the sides and extra tables along the rear. Business appeared to be good enough, with plenty of customers at the tables and games. Going downstairs—one flight of which ran from the balcony at each side—they found the busy condition included the long bar.

"I'll go help out," Cromer said.

"Sure," Derringer replied. "Reckon I'll mosey around the games."

Leaving Calamity with Goldie, Derringer accompanied Sharp and Gitsen to the nearest faro table. As far as he could see, the game was conducted fairly. Its dealing box had an open top, always a sign of a straight game, and held new cards.

"We've just had new decks come in," Gitsen remarked. "I'd like to pick up at least another hundred of 'em from Werner. Last time his order to Bletchley's was lost in the mail. I reckon damned near every place in town was using old cards until the new stock came in."

"You're running this end of it, Buck," Derringer confirmed. "Do what you want on it."

While talking, Derringer watched a few plays of the game.* He felt satisfied with what he saw; the dealer made no attempt to alter the run of the cards to favor the house and the case-board—recording the cards played and whether they won or lost—was accurately maintained.

Not far away, at another table, Derringer saw a stud poker game in progress and moved across to watch it. While technically a four-handed private game, a dealer sat at the table to take the house cut from every pot and act as judge on any controversy. Cutting a game by the house, to help defray expenses, was common enough to need no comment. So Derringer might have moved on but for noticing something of interest.

At that moment all four players still remained in the game on the final round of betting. Peering

---

* For a description of a faro game, read *Rangeland Hercules*.

owlishly at his cards, the dude who had attracted Calamity's attention outside Werner's store opened the betting for a hundred dollars. Already the pot held a large sum, showing the deal-bets had been stiff. However, the next man did no more than see and the third folded his hand. That left the last player, a burly miner by appearance, to make his move. Before him showed the queen, jack, nine, eight of diamonds; quite a spread and offering a wide variety of chances in the hole. From the way he saw the hundred and raised it by two hundred and fifty, he must hold a helpful card in the hole.

Despite the fact that he could have at the most three jacks, for his up-cards were only two jacks, a seven and three, the dude saw and raised. That made the other active player toss his cards on to the deadwood. Again the miner saw and raised, acting with complete confidence. Thinking of the cards exposed in the four hands, Derringer expected the dude to at most see the bet. Yet he did more, shoving a three hundred-dollar raise. Derringer frowned, wondering if the man knew how to play poker. Only two other diamonds had been in view and none of the tens. If the miner caught either a ten or diamond, he held a hand which licked the possible three jacks.

"I'll see it," the miner grunted.

"Three jacks," replied the dude, turning his hole card face up.

"Damn it!" the miner spat out. "I thought I'd got you bluffed."

While the dude raked in the pot, adding it to the money piled before him, the cutter gathered, shuffled and dealt the deck after a player had cut them.

"That's the house rule, except in the big game on Saturday nights, Frank," Gitsen explained in a low voice. "He doesn't play hisself and nobody lays hands on the deck long enough to switch in a cold one."

While Derringer approved of the rule, he made no comment. They stood behind the dude in a position where they could see his cards. From all appearances he knew the game and took all the basic precautions. Raising his hole card slightly, he peeked at it while preventing the chance of a kibitzer learning what he held and then accidentally or purposely giving its value away. Only by looking carefully did Derringer manage to see the card. A ten, with a second of them face up. Only one of the other players held an up-card to beat the dude's; the king of clubs lay before an obvious drummer. After a round of betting, the second cards fell and the dude caught his third ten, although the drummer did not improve his hand.

Despite holding by far the most powerful hand on the board, and in contrast to his previous play, the dude bet small. Under the circumstances he ought to have bet high, building up the pot or driving out weak hands that might improve. While the betting went its round, the dude sat back peering as if half blind across the table at the cutter.

Although one player folded, the drummer and the miner, who held two cards to a high flush, stayed with the dude and the third round of up-cards arrived. Six of hearts for the dude, king to the drummer and another suit card to the miner's flush. Immediately, though not so quick as to arouse suspicion, the drummer made a good bet. The dude sat for a moment staring vacantly, then he shook his head and folded the cards without allowing the ten in the hole to be seen.

"I'm in," he said.

A slight frown came to Derringer's face. Once more the man seemed to be breaking the rules of sensible play. Three tens in his hand beat the two kings held by the drummer and enough of the miner's suit had been in play to lessen his chances of making the flush. Yet the card due to the drummer, when it went to the next man, showed he had made a lucky guess as it would not have improved his holdings. Receiving the card ruined the miner's hopes and he threw in his hand, bringing an anguished complaint from the drummer.

"Damn it!" he wailed, turning his hole card and showing it to be a third king. "When I get 'em, nobody stays in to bet."

Signalling to his companions, Derringer drew back from the table and said, "How good's that cutter, Buck?"

"Good enough to handle a game that high," Gitsen replied.

Which meant, as Derringer knew, that the cutter should be able to spot any known method of marking cards during the progress of the game. For all that, Derringer looked around the table. He saw nothing suspicious: no bandaged finger that might conceal a thumb-tack for use in pegging—making tiny lumps on the cards to identify their value—or tell-tale discoloration of a thumb or forefinger that meant the man daubed marks on the cards. There were other methods: "nailing," making tiny scratches with a fingernail; "waving," bending the cards to make identifying curves. However, any cutter skilled enough to handle a high-stake game would be able to detect such moves.

"Something up?" Gitsen demanded, the honor of his department at stake.

"That jasper may just be lucky," Derringer answered. "But I'd like you to hang around and watch his play for a spell. Let me know what you think."

"I'll do just that," the boss dealer promised.

Moving on together, Derringer and Sharp watched the operation of a chuck-a-luck game. From appearances, news of Banyan's death and will must have leaked out to the staff. Interested glances darted from Derringer to where Calamity and Goldie walked among the customers. Catching the gambler's eye, Calamity started to stroll across the room in his direction. Before she reached Derringer a girl stopped Goldie, and Calamity paused to listen to the conversation.

"Gilbert didn't stop long," Derringer remarked, for the lawyer had left as soon as the introductions ended.

"He'll be in for the big game tomorrow night," Sharp replied. "Will you be sitting in? The boss allus did."

"I'll think on it," Derringer answered, glancing toward a black jack table.

Apparently the dealer had put in a call for his relief. Removing his green eye-shield, the man dropped it on to the table. Then he stacked all the money in front of him neatly. Closing his right hand, he dipped it into his pocket to bring out a plug of chewing tobacco which he transferred to his mouth.

"Dealers come on with empty pockets and're searched by Buck if they leave for anything, or at the end of the shift," Sharp commented, following the direction of Derringer's gaze. "Most of 'em've been with us a fair spell, but it pays to watch the new 'n's."

Cheek bulging with the tobacco, the dealer came toward where Derringer and Sharp were standing on his way to the rear exit.

"Been here long, feller?" Derringer asked.

"Two-three days," the dealer replied, continuing to walk forward. "I've got to go out back, Mr. Sharp, something cruel."

Bracing himself on his good leg, Derringer brought up his cane. Pain bit into him, but he thrust the cane's ferrule hard into the dealer's stomach. Taken by surprise, the man let out a gasp which expelled the tobacco from his mouth. Not only the tobacco! Crumpled, somewhat wet, but still identifiable, a ball of money followed the tobacco and bounced almost to Sharp's feet.

Shock and rage twisted at the dealer's face. Then his right hand dropped in the direction of his holstered revolver and he started to lunge forward.

Sharp stood as if rooted to the spot, everything happening so fast that he failed to grasp the implications and react. Or it could be that he wanted to see how his new employer handled such a situation.

Which put Derringer in one hell of a tight spot. Just in time he dropped the cane's ferrule to the floor and supported his weight. If he raised the cane to make use of its secondary function, he stood a chance of his injured leg buckling under the strain. The same applied should he open his right hand, let the cane fall and reach for his Colt. At that moment Derringer wished that he wore his gun with the butt turned forward so as to be accessible to either hand. Only wishing would not save his life.

Even as Derringer prepared to stake his chance on raising and firing the cane-gun, the matter was taken from his hands.

After helping solve the girl's problem, Calamity had moved once more in Derringer's direction. Seeing the start of the trouble, she realized the risk Derringer had taken. Mentally promising to whomp some sense into his fool head if he bust open his wound, she also prepared to lend him a hand. And with Miss Canary that amounted to a powerful piece of help.

Calamity's instincts warned her that using a gun

was not the answer. So close, using a full 3/4-drachm powder charge, even a .36 Navy Colt might drive its bullet clear through the dealer and retain sufficient power to injure somebody beyond him. That let the gun out and she must rely on other means. Her whip offered a more satisfactory solution to the problem. Always inclined to grand-stand a mite, Calamity knew that the whip would be more dramatic; a major point in her decision.

Long before all the thoughts finished, Calamity's right hand closed on and slipped free her whip. Time did not permit anything really fancy, but she figured what she planned would suffice. Back, then around and out snaked the lash, curling about the dealer's neck from behind even as his gun cleared leather. It came so suddenly, and in silence, that he did not realize his danger until it clamped tight on his throat and chopped off his breath.

Heaving back on the handle, Calamity jerked the dealer to a halt and his revolver clattered to the floor. Given that much of a pause, Derringer limped to a table, sat on it and drew his Colt.

"Just stand there, feller," he ordered.

A piece of unnecessary advice under the circum-stances. Half strangled, all coherent thought driven from him by the unexpected assault from the rear, the dealer stood like a statue. Gitsen and two of the bouncers moved forward, the latter closing on the dealer as Calamity freed her whip.

"Now maybe somebody'll tell me what the hell's coming off here," she said, walking forward as she coiled the whip's lash.

"His chewing-tobacco's a mite rich," Derringer replied.

Bending, Sharp picked up the crumpled ball of money. On smoothing it out, he showed two ten-dollar bills to Gitsen and the girl. Anger came to the boss dealer's face and he swung to glare at the man who stood sullenly rubbing his throat.

"You started early," Gitsen growled, and turned to Derringer. "He's not been here long and this's the first night he's worked solo at a table."

"See to him, Buck," Derringer replied. "You'd've caught him at it had you been where I stood. Only he'd likely not have tried it was you on hand."

Accepting the compliment, Gitsen realized that Derringer did not hold him responsible for the dishonesty of the dealer. So he gave orders to the bouncers and they hauled the man toward the rear exit.

"We'll see he's on tomorrow's stage out, Boss," Gitsen said. "Copping from the house that way's a new one on me."

"And me," Derringer admitted. "I saw him palm the money and wondered how he planned to get it by the search. When I saw him stick the chaw into his mouth, I knew. How about that dude in the stud game?"

"I dunno," Gitsen frankly admitted. "He's good and either lucky or—— I just don't know. Tony, the cutter's good and I trust him. He'd've spotted it if the dude was marking the cards."

An interruption came before Derringer could offer any comments or suggestions. The batwing doors swung open to admit a woman followed by six men. With neat precision the men formed a half circle behind the woman and drew their guns. At a sign from her, one of the six fired a shot into the air. That brought every eye to them.

"Everybody stay put!" she ordered. "That way nobody'll get hurt!"

"Damn it to hell!" Sharp hissed, hand freezing clear of his Colt's butt. "There's nobody upstairs to prime the grenades."

Chapter 11

Despite Sharp's gloomy comment, Derringer did not believe the newcomers planned a hold-up. All the men wore the clothes of working cowhands, looked tough, salty and capable. The fact that none wore masks made it doubtful that robbery was their motive. Nor did Derringer believe mere cowhand horse-play lay behind their actions. Sure cowhands played irresponsible tricks when freshly arrived in town, but not such a foolish stunt as entering a saloon in that manner.

And most certainly not when accompanied—led might be a better term—by a "good" woman.

Tall, clad in a blue shirt waist, divided skirt and riding boots, the woman was clearly no saloon worker. Shortish, curly brunette hair clustered about a very pretty face tanned by the elements in a way no saloon-girl ever attained. Yet her rich full figure, shown off to good advantage by the clothes, equalled any woman's in the room.

Complete silence, brought about by Derringer confronting the crooked dealer, and utter lack of movement continued after the warning. Glancing around in a satisfied manner, the woman advanced to the center of the room. She stood for a moment looking around, the heavy riding quirt in her right hand tapping against her thigh. Then she spoke, her voice a deep contralto.

"I'm Sal Banyan," she announced, and waited until the rumble of surprised talk died down. "Seems like my husband got himself killed. From what I hear, he let some tail-peddler sucker him into willing her the place. Well, I'm here to take it back. So if she's down here, that son-of-a-bitching whore'd better run; or I'll drag her out by the hair."

Hot indignation flushed Goldie's face at the insult to her boss' memory and that a "good" woman would have the audacity to come into the saloon. So she started to move forward. Before she could complete a step, a hand clamped on her arm. Turning, she met Calamity's cold-eyed gaze.

"It's me she wants to see," the red-head said quietly, and unbuckled her gunbelt. "Hold this, Goldie."

Having seen that Sal Banyan did not wear a gun, Calamity knew that kind of show-down was out. Never one to ignore a challenge, especially when put in such a manner, she advanced until she stood clear of the crowd.

"I'm her. So get to dragging."

A low hiss broke from Sal's lips and she tensed, her right hand raising. Made from the penis of a buffalo bull dried to pliant hardness, the quirt she held formed a deadly weapon capable of ripping bone-deep through flesh—only Calamity carried the means to copper its threat. With deft ease, the whip's lash curled back ready to strike. Seeing it, Sal stopped her movement. Long before she could reach the other girl and use the quirt, the bull whip's lash would be biting at her.

"That's how it is, huh?" Sal hissed.

"Throw your quirt over the bar and my whip goes after it," Calamity answered. "Either that or I'll take your legs from under you."

"How do I know you'll get rid of the whip after I've thrown it?"

"Those six yahoos behind you'll see to that. Come on, big mouth, make your play. Throw the quirt over the bar and then we'll see who gets hauled out by the hair."

Maybe hot temper had caused Calamity's original acceptance of the challenge, but already controlled thought had returned. The six cowhands behind Sal could only be removed by gun-play the way things stood. If something happened to take their attention and hold it for a spell, Derringer could likely think up a notion to turn the tables on them. Calamity reckoned she ought to be able to supply the diversion, if Sal took the counter challenge.

"What'll we do, Frank?" Sharp breathed.

"Let Calamity make her play," Derringer replied. "Those cowhands'd stop us doing anything else."

Tense expectancy filled the air as all eyes remained on the two young women in the center of the room. Most of the people present did not know what might be happening, but all figured the following events ought to prove worth watching.

Sensing that all the crowd were eagerly awaiting her decision, Sal made it. In the face of Calamity's counter-challenge, she could not back down even if she wished to do so. Not that the thought of backing down entered her head. Like Calamity, Sal had gained something of a reputation as a fighter and knew she could never face her ranch crew if she gave way. Nor could she pretend that throwing away the quirt left her unarmed against Calamity's whip. The six men at her back would make sure that the other girl kept her word. So Sal hurled her whip across the bar. Glass shattered as it struck a bottle.

"All right!" Sal said. "Now you."

Without hesitation Calamity tossed her whip to Goldie who started to coil its lash. Hardly had the whip left Calamity's hand than Sal flung herself forward. A flat-handed slap caught Calamity's cheek, sending her staggering and giving warning of the other's strength. Hurling after her, Sal drove fingers into red hair and bore Calamity back on to a table. An instant later Sal's Stetson sailed into the air and Calamity's hands dug into her brunette curls. Pain and sheer instinct made Sal force herself upward, landing on Calamity's body.

To the accompaniment of excited yells from the crowd, the two girls rolled across the table. It collapsed under their weight, dumping them on to the floor where they churned over and over in a tangle of flailing arms and thrashing legs. Still clinging to each other, they made their feet and reeled around. They tore at hair, lashed slaps and punches, hacked wild kicks at shins, squealing, cursing, gasping.

There was nothing scientific about the fight, just enraged women's tactics pure and simple. Most of the customers had seen hair-clawing tangles between saloon-girls at one time and another. Yet Calamity and Sal put on a brawl that made such spats fade into insignificance. The average saloon-girl's way of life did not keep her fit or allow for prolonged exertions before lack of breath caused her to quit. Not so the two women battling in the Harem. From the start Calamity felt the power of Sal's muscles, the hard firmness of her gorgeous body and knew she had met somebody almost as strong and tough as herself.

For five minutes without a pause the girls went at it, first on their feet, then thrashing around on the floor. Neither gained any advantage that could be held. Each made the top for a time, only to be rolled over, pinned down until she again reversed the position.

Through it all, the crowd gave wild encouragement. Games were forgotten, discussions left unfinished, drinks ignored. At any other time a woman in Sal's position, left recently widowed and trying to regain her husband's property, might have gained the crowd's sympathy; but her speech on arrival had robbed her of it. So only the six men at the door yelled for her, keeping their positions

covering the room, and the support for Calamity
almost drowned them out. On other occasions
when she had tangled in a saloon, Calamity's opponent had always been one of the girls. So, if she
could have heard it, the vociferous acclaim and advice from the female employees might have amused
her.

"Snatch her bald-headed, Calamity!"

"Kick her teeth in, red-head!"

"Rip her apples off!"

Oblivious of the suggestions, although at various times she seemed to be following all three,
Calamity fought on. Somewhere along the line Sal
lost most of her shirt waist, the remains trailing
from her waistband. Then she rose, standing in
front of Calamity, lashing kicks at the red-head's
shins. Pain caused Calamity to draw back her feet,
but Sal clung hold of the back of her shirt and
dragged it from the pants. Feeling her arms becoming entangled, Calamity wriggled back out of
the shirt and staggered clear. The sleeveless undershirt she wore left little to be imagined of what it
covered. Not that she gave a thought to her appearance. Leaping forward, she gave Sal a push
which sent the brunette reeling. Unable to stop
herself, Sal dropped the shirt and sprawled face
forward across a table. Forcing herself up, blood

splashing from her nose on to the green baize, she caught hold of a whiskey bottle by the neck. As Calamity came at her, Sal smashed the bottle on the table-top and lunged.

Wild with fighting-rage Calamity might be, but she could still think well enough to realize the danger. Twisting aside, she missed the jagged edges of the bottle as they sought for her face. Out drove her fist, catching Sal in the cheek hard enough to send her sprawling away but she retained her hold on the broken bottle.

"Nobody move!" yelled the center man of the cowhands, his revolver making a warning arc. "This's between them two."

Even as Derringer decided to take a chance, Calamity solved her own problem. Darting forward, she bent and snatched up her shirt. Then she swung and hurled it at the charging Sal. Opening out in the air, the shirt enveloped Sal's head and she clawed at it with her left hand. Calamity followed it up, grabbing Sal's right wrist and raising it to her mouth. A screech broke from Sal as Calamity's teeth sank into her forearm. Involuntarily she opened her fingers and the glass fell to the floor. Tearing the shirt from her face and hurling it aside, Sal transferred the fingers of her left hand to Calamity's scalp. To Calamity it felt as if the top of her skull was bursting into flames. She opened her mouth to screech and Sal thrust her away, staggering back when releasing the red hair.

"We've got to stop 'em!" Derringer muttered thickly.

At his side, flushed with excitement, Goldie turned toward him. "They'll stop themselves soon enough."

That seemed to be the case. Staggering on their feet, the two girls went for each other again. How it happened nobody could say for sure, but Calamity somehow managed to catch Sal around the knees. Bending so her shoulder rammed into the brunette's mid-section, Calamity acted on sheer, blind impulse rather than conscious thought. Still holding the legs, she straightened and tipped Sal over her shoulders. Horsewoman's instincts partially saved Sal, allowing her to lessen the force of her landing. Desperately she drove up her right leg in a kick as Calamity stumbled and seemed on the point of falling backward on to her. The toe missed, but the shin collided with Calamity's ribs hard enough to knock her away.

Sobbing with pain, exhaustion and fear, Sal dragged herself up and headed for the bar. Calamity had prevented herself from falling by resting her hands on the top of a table. Hearing the yells of warning, she looked around and realized what Sal aimed to do. Behind the bar lay the quirt. If Sal laid hands on it, she could cut her opponent to pieces.

Fighting down the nausea and exhaustion that filled her, Calamity went after Sal. The brunette's legs buckled, but her arms hooked on the bar and she started to drag her aching body upward. Then she felt hands grip her skirt and faintly heard the material tearing. Despite her struggles to avoid it, her feet sank back to the floor. Fingers gripped her shoulder, turning her around. A fist drove into her stomach with sickening force. She tried to scream, but no sound left her tortured lungs. Gagging in agony, she doubled forward. Still the torment did not end. Calamity caught the brunette hair, hauling Sal erect, and lashed a slap that rocked her head savagely. Four more times Calamity slapped, the sound ringing around the room and drawing gasps of sympathy from the onlookers. Sobbing, moaning, Sal collapsed down the front of the bar to lie in a beaten, crouching heap at Calamity's feet.

As she prepared to launch another slap, Calamity became aware that it would not be needed. Slowly the red mists cleared from before her eyes and she became aware of the mass of pulsating agony that filled her body. She wanted to sink down and sob, but fought off the spasm. Sal lay beaten, but there was something more that must be done.

Bending, Calamity dug her fingers into the brunette hair, using it to haul the other girl erect. With one hand still in the hair and the other holding Sal's waistbelt, Calamity began to hustle her across the room. Stepping on the trailing remains of the divided skirt, Calamity completed its destruction and left Sal clad only in her underwear. The cowhands scattered as the women approached and Calamity used almost all her last dregs of strength to propel Sal through the door. Reeling blindly across the sidewalk, Sal ran up against a verandah support post. For a moment she clung to it, then slid forward, down from the sidewalk and landed on the street. An interested spectator had watched the fight through one of the front windows, but withdrew hurriedly as Calamity brought Sal toward the doors. Standing in the shadows at the end of the building, the onlooker saw the brunette's eviction yet made no move to approach her, standing instead as if waiting to make sure that Calamity did not follow her out.

Calamity had no intention of doing so. Knowing Sal to be licked, she stood on spread-apart legs and looked defiantly at the brunette's men. Hair like a wet, dirty wool mop, face streaked with dirt, sweat and nose trickling blood, she showed signs of the exhaustion welling up over her. Yet she kept her feet, oblivious of the fact that her undershirt had ripped down the front and concealed nothing. Her breasts rose and fell as she dragged air into raw lungs. It was a sight calculated to turn even a confirmed woman-hater from his ways; and the cowhands could not be classed as that. Already their revolvers began to sag and their eyes bugged out as they stared their fascination.

"All right!" she said, dragging each word out with an effort. "Put up the guns. Then either go spend some money at the bar or get the hell out of here."

"Just like the lady says, gents!" called a voice from the right side of the balcony.

Looking up, the cowhands saw a deputy sheriff presenting them with a real effective argument in favor of obeying. Tall, gangling, lean as a beanpole and freckled as a turkey egg, with a small chin over a prominent adam's apple, the deputy did not look an imposing specimen—except for what he held. The twin tubes of a ten-gauge shotgun slanted down at the cowhands, handled with a certain competence which proved appearances to be deceptive. At that range, the shotgun's charge could be counted on to spread and sweep the whole group. So the cowhands knew they had no other choice. More so when guns came into the hands of various saloon employees to back Calamity's demand.

"All right, boys," said the cowhand who had acted as their spokesman during the fight. "Leather 'em and let's go get the boss to Doc Fir."

"You licked her fair 'n' square, ma'am," a second told Calamity, and dropped his gun into leather.

On that note the cowhands turned and walked from the room. Silence held for a moment, then Goldie and several of the girls swarmed forward around Calamity. That broke the spell and cheers welled up.

"It'd be best to call for drinks on the house, Frank," Sharp suggested.

"See to it," Derringer replied, and went toward the door as the announcement caused a rush to the bar.

"She's all right, Frank," Goldie said as he thrust through the girls. "I'll get her up to the 'guest' room. She's a mite too tuckered out to make it to the hotel tonight."

Which might have been regarded as an understatement, considering that only being supported by two of the jubilant girls kept Calamity erect.

Derringer knew that he could do nothing to help and so, wisely, stood back to let more capable hands care for the exhausted victor.

"Help her upstairs, you pair," Goldie ordered, and swept the others with a glance. "Go mingle with the trade. Let's keep 'em moving and earn some money."

Prodded into action by their leader, the girls headed toward the crowd at the bar. Music rose, all but smothered by the excited customers' chatter. Half carried by the two girls and followed by Goldie, Calamity disappeared up the stairs and into a room next-but-one to Banyan's private office.

"This here's Like-His Rigg, Frank," Sharp said, coming up with the deputy.

"Tha——" Derringer began automatically, then realized what Sharp had said. "Like-His?"

"Danged fool name," grinned the deputy, obviously used to such a comment. "War baptised 'Orville.' Only when I come West to take this deputy chore folks kept saying, 'He ain't much like his uncle.' You maybe noticed I don't feature Uncle Oscar even a lil bit."

"It don't show much," admitted Derringer.

"Well, folks got around to calling me 'Like-His' and it stuck. Anyways, it's better'n Orville—— Comes to a point, anything's better'n Orville."

Studying Rigg, Derringer decided there was more to him than met the eye. Behind that gangling, slack-jawed exterior lay a real capable peace officer. That had showed in the way he handled the situation; which raised another point.

"How'd you come to be on hand and in the right place, Like-His?"

"Was making the rounds, Uncle Oscar not being back yet. When I heard the ruckus, I just natural looked in through the window to see what I was getting into. Saw enough to figure walking through the door'd get me no place and went round back. Slipped up the stairs and in through Sultan's office——"

"The boss handed keys to the door out to a few friends," Sharp explained.

"Which I'm one of 'em," Rigg went on. "Time I got out there, I saw the gals looked ready to tucker out and waited until they got through afore I billed in."

To attempt anything otherwise would have resulted in shooting most likely. That he had refrained showed further proof that Like-His Rigg knew how to handle a peace officer's work correctly.

"Calamity didn't start the fight, Like-His," Sharp said. "But she sure as hell finished it."

"Sure looked that way," the deputy agreed. "Well, I'd best mosey along and ask them cowhands what their intendings might be."

"If you need any help——" Derringer offered.

"Reckon they'll show more respect for the law happen they don't figure it's tied in with this place," Rigg interrupted. "You'll be Mr. Derringer, I'd say. Doc Fir told me about you. Waal, I'll just say 'Hallo and see you around.' "

"Don't let his looks fool you, Frank," Sharp warned as the gangling deputy ambled from the room. "He's real smart and no slouch with a gun."

"That figures," Derringer answered. "Lord, Sultan sure picked a mixture for his wives."

With the free drinks dispensed, the saloon staff set to work making sure that the night's profits increased to cover the expenditure. Following Goldie's orders, the girls were already mingling with the customers. At a signal from Gitsen, the various operators returned to their games. Catching the eye of the poker game's cutter, Derringer gave a quick inclination of his head.

"Howdy, Mr. Derringer," the man said, sauntering over in a casual manner. "That dude with the blinker's got me worried same as you. I reckon I know every way of marking cards in the game and I'd swear he's not using any of 'em."

"Know anything about him?" Derringer asked.

Often a house man learned a few details about the players in his game from scraps of conversation made between hands. So Derringer did not feel surprised when the cutter nodded.

"He allows to've come into money back East and headed out here to be clear of his borrowing kinfolk. Flashed a fair-sized wad of money when he started and it wasn't from Michigan."*

"How's he play?"

"That's what gets *me*, Mr. Derringer. He handles his cards good enough to have played plenty. Most times he bets the same way. Then he goes and pulls something you'd expect from a raw greenie. Raises when he should be seeing at most and folding for best; or tosses in a hand that looks good enough to put money on. Only every time he does it, he comes out right."

"Are the others noticing it?"

"None of 'em's spoke about it if they are," the cutter admitted. "Mind you, they're not the best players I've come across."

Glancing toward the bar, Derringer saw the four players setting down their glasses ready to return to their game.

. * Michigan bankroll: Thick hut consisting solely of one-dollar bills.

"Find some excuse to change decks," he ordered, and turned away from the cutter before the dude had chance to see them talking together.

All too well Derringer knew the delicate nature of the situation. Nothing could ruin a saloon's business quicker than falsely accusing customers of cheating. Yet he must learn if the dude was winning by pure chance, or through marking the cards during the play. Let one cheat get away with his games and word would spread, bringing in others to try their luck.

On joining the players at the table, the cutter asked if they wished to continue using the same cards. As he hoped, the losers suggested a change. If the dude had taken the trouble to mark the deck, he showed no annoyance to see his work would be wasted.

"I'll go along with the majority," he said. "Maybe it'll change my luck. I'm getting tired of winning anyway."

Chapter 12

⟋⟍

FRANK DERRINGER FELT PUZZLED AS HE FINISHED dressing in Sultan Banyan's living quarters above the saloon. Looking to where a deck of cards lay on the table, he frowned and picked them up.

After the exchange of decks the previous night, the poker game had gone on as before. Although Gitsen had brought the cards used in the earlier part of the game, Derringer had found no time to slip away and examine them. First one thing then another had claimed his attention. Customers wanted to discuss the fight, comparing it with other noted female brawls. Derringer had often noticed the number of people who claimed to have witnessed any event of note. Two of the crowd declared the fight equalled that between three townswomen and several dance-hall girls in Bearcat Annie's Quiet Town saloon.* Having been present in the town at the time. Derringer admitted the two fights came close to equal in ferocity; yet could not remember either of the men being on hand to see the other. Several of the crowd appeared to know of Banyan's death—the fight had prevented it from becoming general knowledge sooner—and requested details. All showed genuine sorrow at the killing and none gave a hint of being actively interested in it.

Despite the change of decks, the dude had continued to play in his erratic, yet successful, manner. Even before he could possibly have marked sufficient cards to gain information, he threw in one hand that looked like a winner and called a bluff against all tenets of sensible play.

Still curious, Derringer asked Gitsen to trail the dude after he left. Eager to clean the possible stain against his department, Gitsen agreed with the suggestion. However, the dude went straight to the hotel and to his room without seeing or speaking to anybody.

As he reached for the cards, Derringer remem-

---

* Told in *Quiet Town*.

bered Calamity. From faint sounds filtering through the party door, he concluded the girl was awake. So he put off the examination and crossed the room.

Lying naked on the bed in the small room next to Banyan's living quarters, Calamity groaned and cursed.

"Am I hurting you?" Goldie asked, gently rubbing the oily liquid given to her by Calamity on to the bruised body.

"No worse'n getting tromped on by a hoss!" Calamity gritted. "Only I'll feel better when you're through."

After attending to the battered Sal, carried to his office by the cowhands, Fir had hurried to the saloon. Despite Calamity's protests, he had examined her and stated that she suffered only superficial injuries. With the coming of morning, a stiff, sore and aching Calamity had asked Goldie to help her.

The application of the oil, supplied to her by an Indian medicine woman, made Calamity feel somewhat better. Wincing a little, she sat up and reached for her clothes. A knock sounded at the door leading into Banyan's room as she donned a pair of Indian moccasins.

"Come in!" she called and Goldie left by the other door.

"Hey there," Derringer greeted, entering. "How is it?"

"I never felt better," Calamity answered with a wry grin. "That was one tough gal. Where's she at?"

"The deputy dropped by to say her crew took her along when they left town. Say, Harve Cromer allows that's the best night's business the bar's done in a coon's age. He wants to know if you and her'll tangle every night."

"You can tell him to go stick his bung-starter up his butt, blunt end first!" Calamity growled, touching her discolored left eye gently. "I tell you, I don't even want to tangle with her once a month. Say, is she for real another of ole Sultan's wives?"

"Fir allows she is. Says him and Wendley met her while they were hunting up north of here with Sultan. He married her after only two days, stopped off up there for a spell, then came down without her."

"Why?"

"Sultan never said and they didn't ask," Derringer replied. "Where in hell do you reckon you're going?"

"Down to the hotel, then to see to my team," Calamity answered. "Reckon I'll stick with my room down there for a spell, Derry."

"Don't you trust me?" he inquired.

"With that leg of your'n, what's to trust?" she countered. "Nope, I reckon to stay down there and keep an eye on them three wives. I can't see that Rachel, for one of 'em, just sitting back and letting us take something she figures to be her'n from her."

Walking a mite slowly and with a limp, Calamity left the room. She wished to avoid attracting attention and so kept to the rear of the buildings. At the hotel she started along the alley to the front entrance. Approaching a partially open window, the sound of voices brought her to a halt. Normally she would have ignored a private conversation, but the first words to reach her ears warned that the one inside the room must not be missed.

"You're sure Derringer didn't catch on?" asked one speaker.

"Naw," replied another confidently; both being male voices. "He watched me for a spell, then went off. Most likely the fight made him forget it. Anyways, to make sure I acted agreeable when they wanted to change decks. Not that changing 'em made any difference, heh, Ted?"

"It sure as hell wouldn't," replied the first speaker, and Calamity could sense a self-satisfied grin playing on his face.

"How about that gal?" asked the second man. "Do you reckon she remembers us from Tribune?"

"I don't reckon so. Hey! Shut the damned window. Somebody might hear us."

"I can't sleep with it "closed"—— All right, so I'm not asleep now. I'll close it."

Ignoring the twinges of pain sudden movements caused, Calamity backed hurriedly and silently along the alley. She could guess at the identity of the speakers and did not wish them to know she had overheard their conversation. In fact, for them to become aware of her presence might prove dangerous in view of what she had heard. Just as she reached and started to turn the corner she saw a head poke out of the window. Fortunately it faced toward the front of the building and before it turned she had passed out of sight.

"Now what the hell was all that about?" she breathed, walking toward the alley at the other end. There was no point in returning to the window. With it closed she stood little chance of learning more and might be caught trying to listen. "I'll tend to my team, then go ask Derry what he thinks."

With the work on the six horses completed, Calamity returned to the saloon. She found Derringer talking with Gilbert. Clearly the conversation had come to an end, for the lawyer left.

"He was just asking about last night," Derringer explained as the girl joined him. "Reckons we ought to give an accounting through him to the wives on how we're doing. I agree. Is that all right with you?"

"Sure. Say, let's go upstairs. I've heard something you can maybe make a mite clearer for me."

Going up the stairs, she repeated the conversation overheard at the hotel. When she mentioned the identity of the speakers, Derringer showed visible interest. As soon as they entered Banyan's office and closed the door, Derringer pointed to the deck of cards on the table.

"I was just fixing to look them over," he said. "Only Gilbert sent word up that he wanted to see me."

Before they could say more, a knock at the door prevented conversation. On opening it, Calamity found a wizened old swamper outside.

"Brung this magnificating glass for Mr. Derringer," he told her, holding out the object. "Say, that was some hum-dinger, sock-dollager of a fight last night, ma'am."

"Do tell," she replied. "I didn't see much of it."

Chuckling at the comment, the swamper departed. Returning to the table, she watched Derringer with much interest. Taking the deck firmly in his left hand, he rubbed his right thumb across their upper edges. Focusing all his attention on the backs' design, he noticed that instead of maintaining a steady image it varied a little. For all that, the naked eye barely showed the cause of the variation. So he took up the magnifying glass and held it over the cards.

"They're marked, Calam!" he breathed. "Look!"

The design was of two matching flowers, one above the other and the rest of the surface covered with diamonds of equal size, petals, center of flower and diamonds being colored in Bletchley's traditional blue, while the surroundings of the decorations were white.

Following the direction of Derringer's pointing finger under the glass, Calamity saw each flower bore thirteen petals. The one Derringer indicated had a small part of its upper edge filled in with white. Not much and if the naked eye noticed the discrepancy it might have been regarded as no more than a printer's error.

"Could be a mistake," she said.

"It's called shading," Derringer answered. "And it's no mistake. The bottom flower's marked the same way. Then look at the second diamond from the left. It's lost one point. Same at the bottom right. That's so the marks can be seen whichever way the card's being held. First diamond marked means hearts, second clubs, third diamonds and fourth spades. Starting from the top, whichever petal's marked tells him the card's number."

Checking on several other cards, Calamity found what Derringer said to be true. "A man'd need real good eyes to see them marks across a table," she said.

"Not if he knew where to look and wore glasses with strong lenses," Derringer replied. "Only how the hell did he do it?"

"Do what?"

"Switch in this deck. It's ready marked, not done at the table. The only time he got chance to touch the deck was to cut in his turn. The house man shuffles and deals. So he couldn't——Unless——"

"Unless what?"

"Go ask Buck Gitsen for some more of these new decks, Calam, will you?"

"Sure," answered the girl, and left the room.

Standing at the table, Derringer stared at the cards with an air of fascination almost. Improbable though his theory might seem, he felt sure it must be correct. Bletchleys produced only blue-backed cards, so the dude could have brought in his own deck. But he would hardly have been able to switch it into the game due to the house ruling that the cutter shuffled and dealt.

On the girl's return he broke the seals on two of the new decks and examined the cards. By the time he finished with the first he knew that he had called the play right.

"Calam!" he said. "Every damned deck we brought in with us's marked."

"You mean by the folks who made 'em?" she gasped, realizing the implications of the statement.

"I don't reckon so. A big company like Bletchley's wouldn't chance ruining their good name by doing it. But there're crooked gambling supply houses that could handle it. They'd buy the straight cards from Bletchley's and mark 'em easy enough. Then they pack them in a genuine Bletchley box and pass them to whoever gave the order."

"But those cards come to us from the railroad depot," Calamity objected.

"And arrived so late that the box went on the back of your wagon," Derringer pointed out. "Remember how the canopy was open and nothing taken?"

"Yes—— You mean——?"

"They switched the boxes after luring the dog off. It wouldn't take them long and if they'd got hold of a bitch "in" heat, she'd keep the dog away long enough for them to make the switch. If I hadn't come into the yard, you'd never've known he'd gone. Maybe me coming stopped them fastening the canopy down, or it could be they counted on you figuring the dog'd've bawled should anybody be around and'd think you forgot to lash the covers down the night before."

Calamity let out a lurid mouthful of annoyance and slapped a hand against her thigh. "Damn it to hell! Now I know where I saw that dude and Claggert afore. They were with the other loafers standing outside the yard watching us load my wagon to come up here. Let's go get 'em, Derry!"

"How'd we prove it?" he asked.

"Prove——?"

"Sure. Don't forget, we brought in the cards. From what I've seen of Sheriff Wendley and his deputy, they'd need proof, and good proof, before they'd start tossing accusations around. Or afore they'd reckon we acted right by handling it ourselves."

Before Calamity could make further comment, Sharp knocked at the door and looked into the room.

"Undertaker's just come in, Derry," he said. "Edgar Turnbull from the Big Herd's down at the bar asking to see you."

"I'll be right down," Derringer replied.

Throwing an interested glance at the open decks of cards, Sharp withdrew. After warning Calamity to watch her jaw, which brought a blunt answer, Derringer left the office and walked down to the bar. Claggert stood with a tall, neatly bearded and elegantly dressed man. Holding out his hand, the latter advanced to meet Derringer and the girl. Farther along the counter, the dude engaged a bartender in a game of first-flop dice.

"Derringer, Calamity," the man greeted. "I'm Edgar Turnbull. Run the Big Herd. I thought I'd come along and pay my respects. We might be rivals, but that's no reason why we can't be friends. I always was with Sultan."

Transferring the cane-gun to his left hand, Derringer shook hands with Turnbull and nodded in acknowledgment of the saloon-keeper's introduction to Claggert. Calamity favored them both with a friendly smile which was not sincere in the floor-manager's case. However, she acted as charming and demure as a schoolmarm being interviewed for a prosperous position—if one could imagine a schoolmarm standing with a foot on a bar rail, cigar in hand and glass of whiskey ready for drinking. Calamity accepted the smoke and drink from Turnbull, grinning a mite to herself as she sucked in smoke and watched the men waiting for a burst of strangled coughing that would not come.

"I'm damned sorry about Sultan," Turnbull said. "He was a fine man. Making a will like that's just like him though. Will you be keeping open today, or closing until after the funeral?"

"The boss always said we should stay open if anything happened to him," Sharp put in.

"It was in his will too," Derringer went on. "So we'll be open tonight."

"Then we can hold our regular Saturday night game here?" Turnbull asked. "I reckon Sultan'd want that and it'd be a tribute to his memory."

Listening to the words, Derringer felt a slight tingle of expectation run through him. Financing a deal like the business with the marked cards would come expensive and require the right contacts. It seemed hardly likely that an outsider could pull it off. Nor did Claggert strike Derringer as possessing the planning ability and money to organize it. Should the game succeed, the profits would be enormous. Sufficient of the new decks would be in use around town for a man who knew their secret to clean up.

There might also be a chance of nipping the game in the bud if tilings went as Derringer expected.

"What game's this?" he asked.

"Didn't Sultan mention it to you?" Turnbull said. "Every Saturday four or five of us, Lawyer Gilbert, Colonel Forgrave from the Fort, the banker, Sultan and me mostly, got together here for stud. It'd be your kind of a game, sky's-the-limit and real hot competition."

"I'd count it as an honor to be asked in," Derringer stated.

Just as he expected, Derringer saw the dude coming along the bar toward them.

"Excuse me, gents," the man said, smiling in a winning but apologetic manner. "I couldn't help overhearing your conversation. I hope you don't mind me billing in on it."

"Feel free," Derringer replied.

"I heard you say there's a no-limit game coming off here tonight," the dude continued. "Would I be out of line to ask if there's a chance of sitting in?"

"We play kind of high, mister," Turnbull warned.

"That's how I like it," the dude assured him. "And I can afford it now my rich uncle died and left me all his money."

Derringer admitted that the thing was well done. Without his suspicions, he would probably have been taken in by the dude's performance. After telling of his inheritance and reason for coming West, the dude bought drinks and generally made himself pleasant. Obtaining permission to sit in on the big game, he returned to the waiting bartender. After a little more talk, Turnbull and Claggert left.

"Let's go upstairs, Calam," Derringer said and started to do so.

"What's up?" she asked as they entered the office, for she had caught the excitement in his voice.

"There's a chance we might nail their hides to the wall tonight," Derringer told her. "It'll be risky as hell—— So risky that I don't know if I should ask you to lend a hand."

"You need me?"

"I need help and I'd's soon not ask anybody from the saloon."

Something in Derringer's manner warned Calamity that considerable danger might be involved in whatever he was planning. If anything, the knowledge strengthened her intention of taking a part in the scheme.

"Tell me what you want and I'm damned if I don't give it a whirl," she said.

Chapter 13

WHILE NOT A GIRL GIVEN TO WORRYING ABOUT THE future consequences of her actions, Calamity could not help feeling a touch concerned as she listened to Derringer's plan. All too well she could imagine the penalty if anything went wrong. Which did not mean that she refused to help. Risk or not, she aimed to go through with her part in the affair. So she listened attentively as Derringer went through every detail and asked for him to repeat the instructions which applied to her. Not until certain she knew exactly what to do did she relax.

"I can handle it," she stated. "Do you want me to stick around for anything right now?"

"Not unless you want to," Derringer replied.

"I've got a few things to do around town," Calamity said. "So I'll mosey off and do 'em. See you when I get back."

If Derringer had realized the nature of the "things" commanding Calamity's attention, he might have raised objections. Having learned where to find all the wells around town, she planned to visit them. Figuring that Derringer's male ego would stand edgeways at the thought of a mere girl taking such a risk, she omitted to mention her plans.

Visiting the owner of the first well, she set about the business with typical Calamity efficiency. Under the pretense of looking for a site on which Killem could erect a depot for his outfit, she asked about the problems in sinking a well. Not only did the owner answer her questions but also allowed her to examine the well's shaft while explaining various points. From what she learned and saw, Calamity concluded that was not the well in which Banyan had hidden the Russians' jewellery.

All her other inspections proved equally fruitless. In every case her charm and ability to get on with people paid off and the story of Killem's proposed depot did the rest. With a skill many a trained interrogator would have envied, she extracted information from the unsuspecting owners

of every well. The sum findings proved to be negative. Every well had been dug by its owner, on his
arrival in the town; which seemed to rule out the
possibility of Banyan selecting it as a hiding-place.
Nor could he have hidden the jewellery without
the owner being aware of the fact. From the easy
way every owner answered her questions, she
doubted if any knew Banyan's secret.

With night coming on, Calamity headed toward
the saloon. A thought struck her as she arrived at
the building. On entering, she went down into the
storage cellar. Carved out of the solid rock, it appeared to stretch under the rear half of the bar
room. However, there was nothing in it that might
possibly be called a well.

"Calam gal," she said, walking back to ground
level. "Could be old Sultan was just rambling."

With that she left the cellar and went up to Derringer's room. On arrival, she found the door
locked. Derringer opened it at her knock and allowed her to enter.

"I didn't want anybody walking in and seeing
what I'm at," he said.

One glance at the table told Calamity why.
Walking over, she looked down in an interested
manner at it. Two complete poker hands lay on the
table and six pairs of cards.

"Why six?" she asked, realizing their function.

"I'm not sure how many players there'll be," he replied. "That's something else you'll have to help me with."

Much thought had gone into the selection of the hands and even more to picking the apparently unconnected pairs. Considerable experience in gambling helped with the latter. During lunch with Sharp and Gitsen the talk had turned to the forthcoming poker game. Clearly considering the honor of the Harem to be at stake, in addition to their employer's finances, the two men had given willingly of their knowledge. Keen and able poker players, they knew how best to help Derringer. So they had described how each of the regular players handled his game.

From all he heard, Derringer concluded that he would be up against poker wolves, not rabbits. Not a comforting thought in view of what he had in mind. Yet in a way the skill of the opposition helped. One of the first attributes which led a poker player up from "rabbit" to "wolfdom" was the ability to throw in a worthless hand. Within certain bounds, a "wolf" could be relied upon to react in a certain manner; whereas a "rabbit" stayed in with cards no matter how unpromising.

Telling Calamity what he wanted her to do first, Derringer repeated her instructions for later in the game. Nor did she object to the repetition considering the stakes they were playing for.

At eight o'clock Calamity stood on the balcony and looked down across the crowded, busy saloon. Already the players in the game were starting to gather about the table set up in a well-lit rear corner. Caillard, the banker, stood introducing the dude to Lawyer Gilbert and Colonel Forgrave, a tall, lean, tanned cavalry officer. Leaving Claggert at the bar, Turnbull crossed the room to join the others and they took their seats around the table. That was what Calamity had been waiting for and, after watching them sit down, she went into the office. Derringer stood by the table, ready dressed in his cutaway jacket and a new pair of trousers, with the cane-gun leaning against a chair and his Colt in its holster.

"You've got Gilbert next to you on the left," Calamity said. "Then the soldier, the dude, then Turnbull and the banker at your right."

"Just the six of them?"

"That's all. Claggert come in with Turnbull, but he's over at the bar and don't look like he's fixing to play."

"Go keep an eye on things while I get ready," Derringer ordered, reaching for the cards on the table. "Let me know if anybody else sits in."

Before Calamity reached the door, Derringer had slipped two of the pairs of cards on to the bottom of the deck. Then he placed two more pairs at his left, followed by the lower ranking of the complete hands. The remaining two pairs came next and the second complete hand finished the circle. Picking up a card from each pile in rotation, he gathered them in and placed them on top of the deck.

Made by a tailor who specialized in outfitting professional gamblers, Derringer's jacket had a small pocket not normally found in conventional suits. Situated just inside the left flap, it offered a convenient hiding-place for a small pistol or a deck of cards. For the first time since buying the jacket, Derringer made use of the pocket. Slipping in the deck of cards, he made sure that he could extract it easily and unobtrusively. Satisfied that he could do so when the time came, he walked out of the room and down the stairs.

Approaching the table, he saw with relief that no fresh players had joined the game and the men remained in the places Calamity reported. The girl did not follow him to the table, for her part in the work ahead would come later.

"Sorry I'm late, gents," Derringer said, approaching the table. "The bandage on my leg came loose and I had to fix it."

"Is it all right now?" Turnbull asked.

"Sure. Are you gents ready to make a start?"

"Ready and r'aring to go," Caillaird answered and nodded to the vacant chair. "Sit in and get your feet wet. Do you know everybody, Derringer?"

After being introduced to Colonel Forgrave and the dude—who went by the name of Woodley—Derringer took his seat. Resting his cane-gun against the chair, he lowered himself down awkwardly. In doing so, his right hand flashed across to extract the cards. Without any of the others becoming aware of it, he transferred the deck from the pocket to a place of concealment beneath his left thigh. At that moment receiving the wound proved to be an advantage, permitting a certain clumsiness without arousing the other players' suspicions.

"It'll be good to play with a new deck again," Gilbert commented, breaking the seal and opening the box of cards placed with other necessary items on the table.

"I sure wasn't sorry when you brought them in, Derringer," Turnbull went on. "My stock had just about run out."

If things went wrong, the words would be remembered and the fact that Derringer had arrived on the wagon which brought in the new cards given a sinister meaning.

So far, however, nobody attached any importance to the saloon-keeper's words and the game commenced. The cut gave Gilbert the deal, a fact Derringer considered to be advantageous. During the five hands before the deal reached him he could study his opponents' play and establish certain traits of his own.

Dropping his left hand below the level of the table he saw watchful eyes follow the move. Although he had a reputation for straight dealing, none of the players knew him personally. So they stayed alert and cautious; a point he expected and prepared to counter. Again the wound would be of assistance.

"Damn it!" he said, scratching at his thigh. "Why does a wound always itch when it's healing?"

"They say it's the flesh knitting together causes it," Caillard replied.

Derringer's explanation of his actions seemed to satisfy the others. Provided he did not overdo it, he could lower his hand out of sight without arousing comment or suspicions.

Before the first hand ended, Derringer knew that Sharp and Gitsen had given him true information.

Every man around the table definitely classed as a "wolf." For his part, he took the opportunity to pave the way for later actions by betting high when holding cards which justified such play. At the same time he kept an unobtrusive watch on Woodley and noticed that the dude still showed the same apparently uncanny judgment.

Following her part of the plan, Calamity stayed away from the table. She mingled with the customers, but never so far away that she could not see how the game was progressing. When Caillard gathered up and started to shuffle the cards, she knew the time to take her part was drawing near. Crossing to the bar, she attracted Cromer's attention. He came toward her, walking in a peculiarly strained manner.

"What's up?" she asked.

"Frank told me what you said for me to do with my bung-starter and I did it," he replied with a grin. "What can I get for you?"

"That's what I like, loyal hired help," grinned Calamity. "Put up a round of drinks for the big game, Harve. I'll take it to 'em. You never know, I might get a big tip."

Although nobody could have guessed from his expression, Derringer felt a touch nervous as he watched Calamity approaching with the tray of drinks. He completed his low-wristed riffle-stack shuffle that prevented any chance of the other players seeing the bottom card and placed the deck down for Caillard to cut. The vital moment had come. If anything went wrong, if what came next should be discovered, neither Calamity nor he could expect mercy. There would be no credence given to an explanation of his motives, even if time be granted to make them. The bare facts would appear sufficiently damning for summary justice to be inflicted. Yet he knew he must go on with the plan.

"Damn this leg!" he growled, dropping his left hand as Caillard completed the cut and shoved the cards in his direction.

Alert for the signal, Calamity brought off her part as if she had rehearsed it for days in advance. Letting out a lurid curse, she pretended to slip. The tray fell, striking the floor with a considerable clatter and clashing of glass. At the table everybody but Derringer swung to look at the cause of the commotion, just as he relied on them doing.

Like a flash Derringer's right hand scooped the deck from his table and dropped it into his jacket's outside pocket. At the same moment his left hand slipped under his thigh to fetch out the prepared cards. Before any of the others turned their attention back to the table, the substitution had been made and the cold deck lay where Caillard had placed the other.

"Damn and blast it!" Calamity spluttered, glaring furiously from the damage to the watching men. "This son-of-a-bitching waiting on table's a heap harder'n it looks."

"Serves you right for doing the help's work," Derringer answered. "Don't it, gents?"

"You want to take for the glasses out of Calam's cut of the profits, Frank," Turnbull suggested, and all grinned at the girl's pungently obscene reply.

Coming up with bucket, brush, scoop and sawdust, a swamper started to clear away the mess. However, dedicated poker players never allowed minor distractions to take their attention from the game for any length of time. After the two comments, they turned back to their cards.

Picking up the deck, from which he had taken his hand immediately after placing it in position, Derringer began to deal. Nobody raised objections and he knew the switch—by far the most dangerous moment of his plan—had gone unnoticed.

Out flipped the hole cards, with Woodley watching them fall and reading their value. Four of hearts to Gilbert, jack of spades for Forgrave, ace of clubs to himself, five of hearts to Turnbull, nine of diamonds to Caillard and queen of clubs to Derringer. The first up-cards followed and the opening betting began.

"Ace to bet," Derringer commented.

"She's away for a hundred," Woodley answered, having received the ace of diamonds as the first of his up-cards.

"I'm out," Turnbull grunted, as any "wolf" would when faced with the five of hearts and ten of spades. The chances of improving on such holdings were so astronomically high that only the rawest "rabbit" would stay in a pot with them.

"And me," Caillard went on, folding his cards. A hand of nine and deuce not even the same suits did not rate worthy of attention as third man to bet.

"Reckon I'll have to see that," Derringer said, the king of clubs showing.

"I don't think you're trying," Gilbert sniffed, sending the nine of spades and four of hearts into the deadwood.

For a moment Forgrave hesitated—and Derringer held his breath. If the officer should stay in despite having no more than the deuce of hearts and jack of spades, the entire deal would be ruined. Derringer knew he could never get away with dealing from the bottom in that class of company.

While a "rabbit" could only rarely resist playing in every pot, Forgrave had left that stage of development far behind him. Despite there being only two other players left, he did not consider jack-deuce of different suits offered hope of development. So he did the sensible thing and folded.

"Only the two of us left, Mr. Derringer," Woodley stated unnecessarily as he received the queen of diamonds for his next up-card and looked at the jack of clubs joining the king of that suit before Derringer. "Let's make it interesting and play for two hundred."

"Your two and up two," Derringer said calmly.

"I'll cover the two and raise it two more," Woodley countered.

"Which's supposed to scare me out," Derringer remarked. "All right, that two and up five hundred."

Interest showed on the other players' faces and they studied the two hands, trying to calculate what the hole cards might be. Each hand offered a number of possibilities. So the four men sat tense and expectantly waiting to see what would come next.

"Ace for you," Derringer declared, sending the ace of hearts to Woodley, then turning up his card. "And a little jack of hearts for me. Two aces to bet."

"One bullet kills each of your jacks. Let's bury 'em with five hundred."

Sound play under the conditions. Even if the third ace did not lie in the hole, a wise man would try to scare off his opponent before the pair of jacks could be improved on. That was the conclusion drawn by the four watchers. Woodley knew that all Derringer held was the pair of jacks and receiving the second of them ruined his chances of making a flush. So the dude did not hesitate to reraise when Derringer covered the bet and raised it by the same amount.

In a silence that could be felt almost Derringer dealt the last of the up-cards. Eight of hearts to Woodley and the king of hearts to himself. Nobody spoke for a moment, then Derringer made the announcement.

"Two pair to bet. If you've got 'em, play 'em, I always say. Let's see how a thousand looks for starters."

"It looks good—for starters," Woodley admitted. "So I'll just see it—and raise you the same."

"You're scaring me," Derringer announced. "So much that I'll just cover that thousand and bury it under another five."

While Derringer counted out the necessary amount of money—in hundred-dollar bills brought from the bank that afternoon—he watched the other players. Such high betting might not be the rule on every pot, but the non-players controlled their growing excitement. No greater breach of poker etiquette could be committed than commenting on the betting or play after folding one's hand. So Gilbert, the Colonel, Turnbull and Caillard kept quiet and watched what went on. The last raise took almost all Derringer's money, but he doubted if the betting would end there.

"Here's the five thousand," Woodley said, confirming Derringer's guess. "I'll raise five more, if you'll take my marker. Mr. Caillard can tell you I've enough in his bank to cover it."

"That's true," the banker agreed, thinking of the ten thousand dollars the dude had deposited with him on arrival in Banyan.

"You're on, then," Derringer accepted and watched as Woodley drew up the necessary paper. "What'll my share in this place amount to, Counsellor?"

Standing watching, Calamity could not hold down a gulp of mingled shock and excitement. While she expected the play to be high, the thought of it reaching such a staggering level had never occurred to her. She saw a flicker of surprise show on the four non-players' faces, but still none of them

commented or offered other advice than Gilbert's
answer to the question.

"I'd say around ten thousand," the lawyer
replied in a low voice.

"Then it's your five and up five," Derringer told
Woodley, going on with the no-limit poker player's
chilling warning, "I'm going to tap you out for
every cent you've got."

Caillard darted a glance at Gilbert, as if seeking
advice on whether the bet were legal or not. However, the lawyer raised no objections to Derringer
staking a half-share of the Harem before a probate
of the will gave him the right to do so.

Sweat trickled down Calamity's back, while she
clenched her hands until they hurt. She sensed
rather than saw Claggert standing to one side,
watching the play with cold-eyed attention. Then
she looked at Derringer, wondering at the icy calm
and complete lack of concern he displayed. Even
knowing that the winning hand lay before her, she
doubted if she could have matched his attitude of
calm confidence.

While Derringer made out and signed a marker,
using the paper and indelible pencil provided by
the saloon for that purpose, Woodley darted a
glance at Turnbull. Possibly only Derringer of the
other players noticed, or attached any importance

to it. Yet that glance strengthened his belief that Turnbull shared Woodley's knowledge of the cards being marked.

Impassive-faced, Woodley returned his gaze to Derringer's cards. A momentary worry gnawed at the dude. Maybe he had made a mistake. Even with the aid of the powerful glasses the marks on the backs of the cards did not show over-plainly across the width of the table.

No. There could be no mistake. Even if he had read the value of the mark on the petals wrong, the fact that the second diamond-shape on the top row of the design lacked a point clearly indicated it to be a club. So the hole card could not be a king to complete Derringer's full house. All he held was two pairs, which Woodley's three aces licked all ways and then back again.

True Derringer had bet like he held the full house, but that proved nothing. A man of his ability would show complete confidence even when making a bluff.

All doubts left Woodley, but his financial standing gave him no alternative in the matter. As a stranger in town, he could not expect to be extended credit. Nor could he ask Turnbull for more money without arousing suspicion. Anyway, a wise player in his position, without the advantage of marked cards, would act as he must. So he made out another marker and dropped it into the pot.

"I don't think you've got another king," he forced himself to say, itching to lay hands on the money he knew to be his. "But I'm feeling generous and'll not take any more off you. I'll see you. Here's another little bullet. You'll need that full house."

"And I've got it," Derringer answered, reaching toward the pot without turning over his hole card.

"But that's the queen of clubs!" Woodley burst out before he could stop himself, finger stabbing toward Derringer's cards.

Just too late the dude realized how damning a statement had been shocked from him. He saw suspicion flare on every face—except Derringer's. There he read only cold, mocking triumph. Somehow, the Good Lord only knew how, Derringer had learned of the cards being marked. More than that, he had used Woodley's own crooked deck to his advantage, for the card he turned over was the king of diamonds.

"Now what made you say th——!" Derringer began, ramming home the knife and twisting its blade.

Throwing back his chair, Woodley lunged erect. His right elbow pressed against his side and a

Remington Double Derringer flicked into his hand from the spring-operated wrist hold-out holster he wore. Hampered by his injured leg, Derringer could not hope to rise fast enough to draw his Colt, or bring up the cane-gun in his defense. Even as Calamity grabbed for her gun, a shot crashed to her right. Lead ripped into Woodley's head, spinning him around with the hold-out pistol slipping from his fingers as he fell. The girl swung her head to see who had made such a timely intervention.

Smoke curled up from the Adams revolver in Claggert's hand as he walked toward the table.

"Figured you couldn't move fast enough to stop him, Mr. Derringer," the Big Herd's floor-manager said, "with that game leg and all."

"Thanks," Derringer replied bitterly, for he had wanted to take Woodley alive and able to answer questions.

A desire to avoid that was the reason for Claggert's intervention. Proving it would be difficult, if not impossible.

Chapter 14

SITTING ON THE BED IN HER ROOM AT THE HOTEL, Calamity Jane thought about the events of the previous night. Although the sheriff had not yet returned—he had sent word in with the undertaker that he and Turk would trail Nabbes and question him on the killing of Banyan, then make other inquiries—Like-His Rigg proved competent to handle the affair. When the deputy asked to be told what happened, Calamity prepared to blurt out the whole story complete with accusations against Turnbull and Claggert. Catching a warning scowl and head-shake from Derringer just in time, she left the explanations to him.

According to Derringer's version, certain incidents caused Calamity and himself to suspect Woodley of cheating. Thereafter he told the truth, except that he left out all reference to Claggert's part in the affair. Fear for himself did not cause the omission. Not knowing if Turnbull had brought backing guns along, Derringer wished to avoid a showdown that might end in gun-play and endanger innocent lives. Besides which, he lacked definite proof against the two men. By pretending ignorance of their part in the plot, he hoped to gain time to gather facts to connect them with it.

Give old Derry his rightful due, mused Calamity, he sure handled the whole affair a treat to watch. To hear him tell it, switching in the cold deck was to try out their theories, rather than toss unfounded accusations against a possibly innocent man. He sounded so convincing that the other players declared he should take the pot, even though winning it by a trick. Although a scowl twisted Claggert's face and he seemed on the verge of protesting, Turnbull gave an almost imperceptible signal which stopped him. The saloon-keeper mastered his emotions well, she had to admit. Only by a tightening of his lips did he show what must have been a whole boiling of anger and disappointment.

So the matter ran its course. Derringer stated

that he would refund Werner's money for the consignment of cards—no great loss considering the value of the pot—and gave orders for all the new decks to be taken out of use immediately. That offered Turnbull an excuse to leave. No honest saloon-keeper, or even a crooked one, would want marked cards in use at his tables. With the killing and Turnbull's departure, the game broke up. Not until the Harem closed for the night, however, did Calamity learn just how Derringer had pulled the trick.

He had used one of the marked decks, except for changing its king of diamonds for one, suitably marked as the queen of clubs, from a straight deck he had in his bag. Then the cold deck did the rest.

The funeral of Sultan Banyan took place at ten o'clock on Sunday morning. Almost everybody in town attended; many out of genuine respect for the dead man, but others in the hope of seeing his four widows. All four attended, dressed in as near mourning as they could manage with their limited wardrobes, but they stood clear of each other. Face showing the marks of the fight, Sal wore a cheap black dress bought from a store in town to replace her ruined garments. Although she glared her hate at Calamity, she neither offered to speak nor resume hostilities.

With the ceremony over, the mourners parted, but there was to be a wake in Banyan's memory that night. Calamity ate lunch with Goldie, Derringer and Sharp. From what she gathered, the wake ought to prove a lengthy affair. So, after eating, she returned to the hotel, meaning to grab some rest.

A knock at the door brought her from her reverie. Crossing the room, she opened up and found Velma Banyan standing outside. While Velma had brought more clothes than any of the other wives, none could be termed suitable for mourning. With the funeral over, she had removed the aids to decorum which had lessened disapproval against her through the ceremony.

"Can I talk to you, Miss Canary?" the blonde asked, darting a nervous glance along the passage.

"Come on in," Calamity replied, wondering if the visit might produce some clue to the reason for Banyan's murder.

Once inside the room, with the door closed, Velma wasted no time in getting down to business.

"Do you know that Rachel intends to contest the will?" she asked.

"How's that?" Calamity countered.

"Take you into court and challenge the validity of the will," Velma explained. "She's sounded me and that fat old hag Joan out about going along with her on it."

"So?"

"So it could cost you your chances of keeping the saloon."

"Sultan's will said we got it," Calamity pointed out.

"Yes," agreed the blonde. "But, like Rachel says, a court'll be sympathetic to three poor, betrayed women like us and figure our claim's stronger than any you've got."

Which, Calamity admitted to herself, might prove true. So she adopted the kind of worried attitude she thought Velma would expect.

"Yeah," she said in a low voice. "The court just might at that."

"There's a way out," Velma stated eagerly.

"How?"

"If Rachel and Joan can't prove they were legally married to Sultan, that would only leave me——"

"And Sal," Calamity went on.

"Her?" Velma sniffed. "She doesn't come into it at all. No, Rachel and that Joan are the only ones you have to worry about. If they were to lose their marriage certificates, they couldn't prove they'd ever been married to Sultan."

"Lose?" Calamity repeated.

"All right, damn it!" Velma hissed. "I'll talk straight. If you steal those two's marriage lines and destroy them, they've no case in court."

"And *you* get the Harem for yourself."

"Me!" Velma yelped, sounding shocked. "I wouldn't want to stop in this dead-and-alive town. All I want is half of the profits sent to me monthly."

Then a knock sounded at the door and alarm showed on Velma's face. She stared around her as if looking for another way out.

"I'll see who it is," Calamity remarked.

"They mustn't find us together," Velma answered.

"Get into the wardrobe there," Calamity told her, pointing to the room's most prominent piece of furniture.

From the speed with which Velma obeyed the instructions, she had been involved in similar situations before. Although probably not because she found herself in a room with another *woman* at an inopportune moment, Calamity guessed as she opened the door of the room. She found Joan outside, exhibiting the same nervousness as shown by Velma.

"I have to see you, Miss Canary," the black-haired woman announced. "Only I'd sooner not talk out here."

"Come on in, then," Calamity replied, stepping aside. "What's up?"

Leaving Joan to close the door, Calamity crossed to lean against the front of the wardrobe. As soon as the woman started to speak, Calamity felt pleased that she had taken the precaution. She wanted to hear what brought Joan to see her before allowing Velma to appear.

"Rachel and that blonde trollop are trying to stop you inheriting the saloon, Miss Canary," Joan said.

Behind Calamity, the wardrobe door shook and she knew Joan's words were reaching Velma. However, she continued to lean, asking the questions Joan expected of her and receiving much the same proposition as that put up by Velma. Deciding she would learn nothing new, Calamity commented on the disposal of the other wives' marriage certificates leaving Joan with the only legal claim against the saloon.

"I certainly don't want to own it!" Joan snorted. "That's the kind of business only a cheap tramp like Velma, or whatever she calls herse——"

Feeling an extra hard push, Calamity sidestepped and Velma erupted from the wardrobe.

For a moment the two widows stood glaring at each other.

"You lousy old bitch!" Velma hissed, and slapped Joan's face as hard as she could swing her arm.

Maybe Velma expected that one slap to end the matter. If so, she received a rapid and painful disillusionment. Gasping with pain, Joan rocked on her heels. Then she whipped her right arm up, slashing the back of her hand into the blonde's mouth. Staggering from the blow, Velma raised a hand to her face. She stared at the red smear of blood on it and let out a screech of rage. Neither woman moved for almost five seconds. Then, as if at a signal, they lunged at each other. Hands dug into hair, tugging and pulling as they spun around with squeals of mingled pain and rage. Tripping, they crashed to the floor still locked together like a pair of bob-cats fighting for a mate.

At first Calamity contented herself with standing and watching the fight. For two women who probably had never been entangled in a hair-yanking brawl, they set about it with considerable gusto. Whatever they did to each other, Calamity figured they deserved it. Then Joan straddled Velma's body, kneeling astride her despite the other's feeble bucking efforts to escape. Gripping the blonde hair, Joan raised and crashed Velma's head against the floor. Desperately Velma raked at the other woman with her fingernails, leaving a bloody scratch down her cheek. Once again Joan crashed the blonde head on to the floor.

"H-Help me, Canary!" Velma croaked.

Suddenly Calamity felt revulsion at the entire affair. No stickler for some conventions, she held firm views on how a wife should behave after becoming a widow. Those two squalling bitches had recently lost their husband and Calamity figured Sultan Banyan rated better than they, or the other two wives, accorded his memory. From all she could see, Calamity concluded that Banyan had seen to his wives' welfare even though separated from them. Yet, with his body only that morning laid in its grave, all at least two of his widows could think about was laying hands on more than their share of his money and cat-clawing each other.

Moving forward, Calamity sank her fingers into Joan's tangled hair. With a heave, she swung the woman upward and pitched her across the room. Sobbing, dazed, but with murder glaring in her eyes, Velma rose.

"Let's tear her eyes out!" she gasped and started toward Joan.

Around lashed Calamity's arm in a slap that knocked Velma spinning on to the bed. Joan thrust herself away from the wall, rushing forward with hands raised like the talons of a striking hawk. Jumping forward, Calamity drove a punch into Joan's belly. Breath burst from Joan and she collapsed, holding her middle.

"Get up!" Calamity snapped, glaring at the two women.

Sobbing, Velma forced herself up from the bed. She turned and looked at Calamity, mouth opening to speak. Then she saw the expression on the girl's face. With a scared croak, the blonde staggered to the door, opened it and fled. Slower to obey, Joan dragged her frame erect. She also realized that discretion was the better part of valor, assuming she could think logically at that moment. Clutching at her middle, she reeled sobbing out of the room.

Standing glaring after the departed women, Calamity waited until the worst of her anger was subsided. Then she stamped across to the door and slammed it. Leaning her back against the wall, she shook her head.

"What's a bunch!" she breathed. "I don't blame ole Sultan for leaving any or all of 'em."

With that she returned to the bed, flung herself down on it and lay thinking about the latest turn of events. All she had learned from the visit was that Rachel intended to fight for the saloon and had tried to recruit two more of the wives in her scheme. Apparently Sal had not been included. When Turnbull asked her, in Calamity's hearing at the funeral, if she would attend the wake, Sal declined and claimed that she intended to ride back to her ranch that same afternoon.

Deciding to tell Derringer of the visits when they met at the Big Herd that evening, Calamity stayed on the bed. A late night and the events of the day added to make her drift off to sleep. When she woke, night had fallen and she knew the time had come for her to attend the wake.

"Miss Canary!" called a voice as she walked toward the Big Herd Saloon.

Turning at the sound of her name, Calamity saw a small, skinny, sly-looking man approaching. He wore town clothes of inexpensive cut and grinned in an ingratiating manner as he stopped before her.

"Howdy," Calamity said, wondering why he had called to her.

"Are you still looking for that place for Mr. Killem?"

"Sure. If I can get what I want."

"You don't know about Sultan Banyan's house, then?"

"What house?" Calamity asked.

"I could lose my job telling you this—" the man hinted.

"Will five simoleons make it easier for you?" she sniffed, taking the money from her buckskin jacket's inside pocket.

"Sure——" he agreed, reaching out a hand.

"When I've heard what I'm paying for," Calamity told him.

"Sultan's got a house on the south-bound trail, half a mile out of town. It'd be just what you want, got a well already dug and all. Trouble is that one of them mine-owner's coming to look it over. The deed to the place's in Mrs. Rachel's name and she's fixing to sell out to him."

"How'd you know all this?"

"I get around," the man answered, glancing about him as if wishing to avoid being seen with the girl. "If the place's what you want, you might get her to sell to you."

"I might at that," Calamity admitted. "Thanks. Here's the five."

Snatching the money, the man shot into an alley and disappeared. Calamity watched him go, frowning a little and wondering what she should do for the best. Wherever he had picked up the information, one point made it worth investigating.

If Sultan owned the house, the Russians' jewellery might be hidden in its well. The thing being, what to do?

If she went to the Big Herd and left it accompanied by Derringer, interest and maybe even suspicion might be aroused. The possibility of somebody else hunting for Banyan's treasure had not escaped Calamity, and could be the reason for his murder. In which case, the less folks suspected the safer for herself during the check on the well. So she decided to go alone.

That brought up another point. Attending the wake did not call for the wearing of weapons. Not openly at any rate. So she had left the whip in her room, along with her gunbelt. However, she carried her Navy Colt in her waistband, hidden by the jacket. The revolver ought to be enough of a weapon in case of an emergency. There would be no need for her to return to the hotel and she did not wish to be too late arriving at the wake in case her absence should arouse comment.

Despite wanting to hurry, Calamity refused to let the need for speed override caution. The idea that she might be walking into a trap had come to her shortly after she had paid for the information. So she kept her hand close to the Colt, while ears and eyes remained constantly alert to warn of lurking enemies.

Nothing happened as she walked along the southern trail. The country bordering it offered scant cover, but as she went farther from town an uneasy feeling grew more intense. Always a fair judge of distance, she realized that at least half a mile lay between her and the town. Yet there was no sign of a house. Any property built by Sultan Banyan would be of imposing size, or she judged his character wrong. Which meant she should be seeing at least some sign of it by that time. At least a quarter of a mile farther on, she came to a halt.

"Damn it!" she breathed. "There's no son-of-a-bitching house out here."

Three possibilities sprang to her mind: first, somebody had lured her out of town to kill or run her off; second, the informant had heard of her supposed search for a property and grabbed a chance of making some easy money by pretending to know of a suitable place; third, it was a practical joke. Of all, she cared for the third least of all. It seemed unlikely that anybody would play a joke at such a time. Yet the lack of attempts seemed to rule out the first choice. Which left the second and Calamity disliked thinking of that.

"Could be he slickered me," she muttered, turning and heading back the way she came. "I'm sure pleased I didn't tell ole Derry about it."

Still fuming and promising herself what she would do when she laid hands on the man, Calamity walked toward the Big Herd Saloon. Considerable noise rose from inside, it having been decided that Sultan Banyan would not want a quiet, tearful send-off. However, Calamity did not reach the batwing doors. The gangling shape of Deputy Sheriff Rigg stepped from a side alley and blocked her path.

"Howdy, Like-His," she greeted. "Going inside?"

"No, ma'am. Just hold it up here for a minute, will you?"

"What's up?" she asked, coming to a halt.

"Where've you been?"

Calamity did not want to admit to Rigg that she might have fallen for an old false-information trick, or go into explanations. Then she noticed how he stood; left hand behind his back, right negligently—too negligently—trailing by his low-hanging Colt. That was the stance of a man expecting trouble and ready to counter it.

"Around," she replied.

"Down to the hotel?"

"No. Just strolling around to check on my hosses."

"Funny, that's the first place I looked for you," Rigg said.

"Now why'd you coming looking for me?" she asked.

"Somebody knocked Mrs. Velma Banyan cold at the hotel. Done stole her and Mrs. Rachel's marriage lines."

"And you reckon I did it?" Calamity snorted. "Hell, that Joan——"

"Yeah, that Joan," Rigg interrupted and brought his hand from behind him. "You recognize these, Miss Calamity?"

"Sure," Calamity answered, looking at the whip and hat he held. "They're mine. I left 'em at the hotel when I come out."

"That's where I found 'em," Rigg said quietly. "The hat was lying by Mrs. Joan's body—and the whip was round her neck."

Chapter 15

SHOCK NUMBED CALAMITY AS THE IMPLICATIONS of the words sank into her head. Tense and alert, Rigg watched her, then went on:

"Woman at the hotel allowed she saw somebody running from Mrs. Joan's room. A gal, wearing man's clothes—buckskin jacket, bandana around her neck, pants, riding boots."

He might have been cataloguing Calamity's wardrobe and she knew it.

"Y-You think that I killed her?" she asked in a voice barely louder than a whisper.

"You'll have to tell me where you've been so I'll know one way or the other," Rigg replied. "Hand over your gun, ma'am."

Despite the shock, Calamity knew better than to disobey. Slowly, using her left hand and avoiding gripping the butt, she took out the Colt.

"Like I said, I was walking," she stated, handing the weapon to Rigg.

"Did anybody see you?"

"Not while I was walking. Only—only the feller who got me to go out of town. He'd know."

"Who was he?" asked the deputy, after Calamity had explained how she had gone on false information to see a possible site for Killem's freight yard.

While Calamity realized just how thin the story sounded, her instincts warned that to tell the real reason for going out of town would be far worse. If she found the jewellery and it could not be returned to its rightful owners, the wives would have claim to it. Which offered a mighty good motive for stealing the marriage certificates, or killing one of the claimants.

"A runty cuss with a weasel's face!" she said. "Looked like a clerk, or some such."

"Could be any one of a dozen fellers around here," Rigg grunted. "I'll see if I can find him, after I've put you in a cell."

"In a ce——!" Calamity gasped.

"Listen, gal!" Rigg said. "I don't know whether

you killed Mrs. Joan or not. But one thing I'm certain sure of. When word gets out, folks're going to figure you'd a reason for doing it. So I want to say I've got you locked up safe until we find out for sure. That way nobody'll start acting foolish or shouting 'hang-rope.' "

Possibly for the first time in her life Calamity knew real fear. All too well she knew the temper of western folk where "good" women were concerned. The evidence against Calamity, though circumstantial, would appear damning. Folks would remember that she and Derringer had shared an inheritance that should, in part at least, belong to the dead woman. So false, but dangerous, conclusions might be drawn.

Briefly Calamity considered flight, but cold logic saved her from the blunder. Rigg would do his duty by stopping the attempt; and even if she made it, running would be regarded as a sign of guilt. More than that: a heated mob might assume Derringer shared her guilt and, if she escaped, vent their fury on him.

One thing more persuaded Calamity to stand her ground. Despite his appearance, Rigg was a smart peace officer, honest and willing to search for the truth. So she went along with him to the jail.

On entering the office through the front door, Calamity looked around. Although little different from any other such place seen in her travels, the office had a grimmer aspect to the eyes of a prisoner. A door opened into the alley on either side of the office, giving a choice of three exits from the room. Beyond the desk were the two cells Banyan City found satisfactory for their limited needs.

Taking the key-ring from the desk, Rigg indicated a cell and, after Calamity had entered, locked the door. Then he returned the keys to the top of the desk and locked her weapons in the side cupboard, the key of which went into his pocket.

"Anything I can do for you?" he asked, walking toward the door.

"Sure. Tell Derringer what's happened," she replied. "I didn't kill her, Like-His."

"I surely hope not, Miss Calamity," he said. "I surely do. I'll tell him right off."

Left alone in the jail, Calamity gripped the bars of the cell and clung to them. Then she regained her self-control. Turning, she went to the hard bunk and sat down. A shudder ran through her as she stared at the bars. Never before had she been confined and she found the sensation unnerving. Fighting down her concern, she tried to concentrate on thinking who might have killed Joan.

Just how long Calamity sat in a half-daze, she could not say. The sight of the front door opening brought her back to reality. Wearing a hooded cloak over her dress, Velma entered the office. She darted to the desk, picked up the keys and walked over to Calamity's cell.

"I've come to help you!" the blonde said, trying a key in the lock. "I heard they'd arrested you for killing Joan. Then Rachel came to see me. She said I should tell the deputy that it was you who knocked me out——"

"Who did hit you?" Calamity demanded, watching Velma try another key.

"I—I don't know. There was a knock at my door. I opened it and the next thing I knew, I was lying on the floor with all my clothes and things thrown all over the room and the marriage lines gone."

"Why're you helping me?" Calamity asked as the lock clicked and the cell door opened.

"I-I'm scared of what Rachel will do to me. You can handle her. You're tough enough to make her leave me alone."

Deciding to make the most of her chance, Calamity left the cell. One glance at the desk told her that she could not hope to force it and obtain her weapons. However, the carbine was at the hotel. So she started making for the right side door as being farthest away from possible witnesses leaving the Big Herd Saloon.

"This way!" Velma hissed urgently, making for the opposite side of the room.

A thought suddenly struck Calamity while following the blonde. What lay behind Velma helping her to escape? Surely she did not think that Calamity could stay in town to protect her from Rachel? It seemed very unlikely. Nor would the blonde be likely to hold kind-hearted feelings toward her after the incident at the hotel.

Reaching the side door, Velma drew it open. Then she paused, turned and looked at Calamity.

"You'd better slip my cloak on," she said. "That way if anybody sees you, they won't recognize you."

Smart thinking—maybe just a mite too smart for a girl of Velma's intellect; although Calamity did not put the thought into those exact words. Every action the blonde made seemed to be part of a careful, conceived plan. Yet the last bit appeared to come as an afterthought; almost as if she had only just remembered it in time.

Suddenly, giving no warning of her intentions, Calamity shot out her hands. Catching Velma by the shoulder, while the blonde was still fumbling with the cloak's fastenings, she turned her and thrust her through the doorway. A frightened gasp broke from Velma and she started to say something. Two shots cracked from the rear end of the alley. Calamity heard the sound of bullets driving into flesh and chopping off the blonde's words. Even at such a moment she automatically noted the shots came from a carbine, not a revolver.

Instantly Calamity slammed the door and closed the top bolt. There was no time to consider that she had sent Velma out to be shot. Everything leapt into focus like the rod of the bolt slipping home. Instead of trying to rescue her, Velma had planned to send Calamity to her death.

Working at racing speed, Calamity's brain saw the plan and realized that the danger had not ended. While outside the cell she could still be regarded as escaping. So she turned and ran back to it. Just as she entered and closed the door, she heard a man's voice outside. The carbine spat again, from nearer the door, followed by the deeper bellow of a revolver. A sharp cry of pain, feminine in its timbre, came on the heels of the second shot and something crashed into the jail's wall. Boots thudded as the man with the revolver ran down the alley toward the side door.

All this registered in Calamity's subconscious

mind as she entered the cell and closed the door. Reaching through the bars, she turned the key in the lock, removed it and tossed the ring on to the top of the desk.

Trying the side door and finding it fastened, the man in the alley ran back the way he came. Calamity saw him pass the front window, then the door opened and he entered. It was Like-His Rigg, face showing bewilderment and strain.

"I heard shots!" Calamity said.

"Yeah!" he replied, crossing to the cell and looking at the key-ring on the desk in passing. "I was coming back here and heard some up the alley. When I got to the comer, I saw Mrs. Velma down and somebody standing over her. So I yelled and—and got shot at. So I cut lose fast—Calamity——— It was that other Mrs. Banyan!"

"Which one?" Calamity demanded, seeing the shock on the deputy's face.

"The one you tangled with at the Harem."

"Sal!"

"That's her. She'd shot Mrs. Velma. Lord! I can still see her sprawled there with her hair all white over her face."

Calamity could see everything. Waiting in the dark at the rear of the building, Sal had shot at the cloaked figure which emerged. In falling the hood had slipped back to show Velma's long blonde hair and tell Sal of the terrible mistake she made. Then she had heard Rigg's voice and either panicked or acted smart. If she had heard the door's bolt go home, she would guess at Calamity's next move. So, instead of receiving acclaim for stopping a jail-escape, she stood a chance of being arrested for murder. Sal would know how damning the appearances must be. Rather than take a chance, she had shot at the deputy and missed.

"Let me out!" Calamity snapped. "One of 'em might talk."

"They won't!" Rigg answered, looking badly shaken. "Mrs. Velma died just as I got to her—and I didn't have time for fancy shooting."

Which meant, as Calamity guessed, that he had shot to kill and succeeded.

"She'd've killed y——" she began.

Slowly the dazed expression left Rigg's face and Calamity saw him making a visible effort to regain control of his shaken nerves. Turning the key in the cell door, he opened it.

"I reckon I called things wrong, Calamity," he said. "Mrs. Sal's wearing a buckskin jacket, bandana, pants and boots too."

"Where's Derry?" Calamity asked as she walked from the cell.

"That's what brought me back here," the deputy replied. "When I got to the Big Herd and asked, damned if I don't get told that Lawyer Gilbert's clerk just a bit back come in to say Calamity Jane'd met with an accident down to the Harem. Now I ain't smart, but that sure as hell didn't sound right to me, seeing's how I'd done got you down here. So I come back."

"Derry's gone to the Harem?" Calamity gasped, making the words more statement than question.

"Him and Gilbert both—— And I minded something else. That there clerk of Gilbert's. He'd fit your description of the feller who sent you off to look for that place real good."

"Damn it, we've got to——" Calamity started.

Then they heard the sound of voices coming from the direction of the Big Herd. Somebody had heard the sound of the shots, possibly thought about it and finally decided to investigate. Once again Rigg proved equal to the occasion. Stepping across to the desk, he opened the drawer and removed Calamity's weapons.

"Here," he said. "You go down there and see if Derringer's all right. I'll stop here and tend to things."

"Thanks, Like-His," Calamity said sincerely, making for the door at the right side of the building. "I didn't kill Joan."

"Right now, that's just what I'm thinking," he replied. "Or I'd not be turning you free."

Slipping out of the door, Calamity darted along the alley. She thrust the Colt into her waistband, retaining the whip in her right hand as the better weapon for use on a dark night. To avoid attracting attention, she stayed at the rear of he buildings during the walk to the Harem. She saw nobody until turning into the alley by the saloon. A light glowed in the barroom, just one lamp, not the whole system of illumination. Starting toward it Calamity saw a shape rise from sitting on the stairs running up to the balcony and first-floor rooms. With a touch of satisfaction Calamity identified the small man whose false information had set her up to be charged with murder and possibly hung.

Clearly the man did not recognize her; a puzzling aspect until she remembered how Sal had been dressed. His opening words confirmed Calamity's summation of the situation.

"That you, Mrs. Sal? The boss and the other's insi—— Hey! You're n——"

Only the discovery came too late. By that time Calamity was close enough to take the necessary action. Gliding forward, she drove the whip up. Its handle—which had looked enough like a carbine's barrel in the poor light to increase the likeness to

Sal—drove butt-first with sickening force between the man's legs. Numbing, unmentionable agony ripped into the clerk, rendering him speechless and without the ability to think. As he doubled over, Calamity raised the whip. She was human enough—and woman enough—to feel satisfaction as the loaded handle crashed down on to the man's head and dropped him unconscious to the ground.

"And that was a good five bucks worth, I'd say," she mused, transferring her whip to the left hand so as to draw the Colt with her right.

Silently she went by the still shape of the clerk, moving toward the side window. Before she burst into the barroom, she wanted to discover what she would be up against. On looking, she saw the wisdom of her caution. Derringer was sitting on the edge of a table, left leg swinging and cane-gun by his right side. For a moment Calamity thought all must be well. Then she saw the menacing way in which Gilbert confronted him. Nor was the lawyer alone with Derringer. Rachel stood at Gilbert's side and beyond her Turnbull glowered from one to the other of them. Adams in hand, Claggert leaned against the bar in a position from which he could cover the gambler.

It all amounted to higher odds than she could buck by bursting in through the front or side door.

Then she remembered something and a cold, hard grin twisted her lips. Turning, she went to the stairs and climbed them fast. On the balcony, she took a key from her pocket and unlocked the door to the private office.

Pausing to ease off her boots, she advanced on bare feet to the safe. The two Ketchum grenades and box of percussion caps stood in their usual position and Calamity's hands went to them. Then she foresaw the difficulty. While Sharp had taught her to prime the grenades, the lessons did not include doing so in the dark.

Turning, she crept silently back to the desk. Cautiously her reaching hands found the lamp on the desk's top and drew it toward her. Then she raised the glass and sucked in a breath. Taking a match from her pocket, she rasped its head on the seat of her pants. As she applied the flame to the lamp's wick, her ears strained for the first warning sound that the glow had been noticed from below. None came and she adjusted the wick to give just the bare amount of light necessary for her purpose.

With even that small amount of illumination Calamity could walk straight to the safe and not worry about colliding with something that might make a noise. At the safe, she placed the lamp on top and picked up one of the grenades. Then she paused to collect her thoughts. One mistake could cause a premature explosion.

"Which won't do Derry any good at all," she told herself silently. "And me a damned sight less."

Taking hold of the base flange, she drew it and the firing plunger from the tube. That left the way clear for inserting the percussion cap. Calamity's hands felt hot, wet, but steady enough, as she moved the deadly little copper cup into place. With it in position the thing in her hands was no longer inert, harmless, but a lethally dangerous explosive device. More so as she eased the plunger rod back up the recess. Pushed too far, it would crush the percussion cap and ignite the charge. If not far enough in, it might slip out or fail to drive home on impact.

Satisfied at last, she glanced at the second bomb and decided not to waste more time. So she went to the door, whip and Colt in her belt, bomb in hand. The same key opened both the room's locks and she turned it. Hardly daring to breathe, praying that the click of the lock had gone unnoticed, she eased open the door. Voices came from below, talking in normal tones. It seemed that nobody suspected her presence, or they concealed it well.

Stepping as if walking on eggshells, she reached the edge of the stairs. Then she remembered Claggert standing at the bar. From the stairs she could not see him, for the balcony extended too far. And Claggert was the most dangerous of them all. Calamity could recall how fast he had drawn and with what little compunction he shot Woodley dead.

Then the matter was taken from Calamity's hand. Looking up, Rachel stared at the stairs.

"Up there!" the woman screamed, pointing. "It's Canary!"

Chapter 16

Just ten seconds too late Frank Derringer realized he had walked into a trap. When Gilbert's clerk came to him at the Big Herd and whispered that Calamity was hurt down at the Harem, Derringer left immediately. Accompanied by Gilbert and the clerk, he went along the back streets to the Harem. Doing so took them by the rear of the jail at the time when Like-His Rigg was escorting Calamity in through the front. The fact that Turnbull and Claggert had left the wake earlier failed to register any alarm for Derringer. To the best of his knowledge, neither man knew that he suspected them of being involved in the abortive marked cards swindle. So he saw no reason to worry over their absence, which could be accounted for in so many innocent ways.

Even the fact that the saloon lay in darkness failed to ring a warning in his haste to learn what happened to Calamity. The clerk could only say that he had found her lying by the open side door and had taken her into the building before hurrying off in search of help.

Leading the way, Derringer walked through the still-open door into the barroom. Although Gilbert followed, the clerk stayed outside and drew the door closed. That was when Derringer began to get suspicious. He sensed rather than saw the other shapes in the room. A shaft of light lanced into his eyes as somebody unhooded the front of a bull's eye lantern.

"Stand right there, Derringer!" ordered Turnbull's voice from behind the light. "Lean on your cane and keep the left hand high."

There could be no arguing with the order under the circumstances, so Derringer obeyed. Standing in such a manner, he could not hope to raise and fire the cane-gun. Even if he did, it held only one bullet and at least two people stood before him. So he kept still and allowed Gilbert to pat over his body in search of weapons.

"He's not armed," Gilbert announced. "I didn't think he would be."

A match rasped and Derringer saw Rachel lighting a lantern on a table. In its glow, Derringer studied the situation. Keeping well clear of the gambler, Gilbert moved around and joined Rachel and Turnbull. The saloon-keeper closed the hood on his lantern and placed it on the table. However, he still held a Colt Pocket Police revolver. Across the room Claggert leaned on the bar, Adams in his right hand and a bottle of whiskey open in his left.

"What the hell——?" Derringer snapped, acting as they might expect him to do.

"We're going to kill you," Gilbert replied. "Upstairs, trying to break into the safe."

"That'll take some explaining away."

"Not so much. Calamity Jane has been arrested for the murder of Joan Banyan and will soon be shot trying to escape. Turnbull and I missed you at the Big Herd and came here to investigate. We found you trying to open the safe, you pulled a gun and we had to shoot in self-defense."

"And Mrs. Banyan there?" Derringer asked, holding down his anxiety for Calamity's welfare.

"Oh, she'll be leaving here as soon as we hear the shooting from the jail," Gilbert replied.

"Doesn't trust you to handle it, huh?" Derringer grinned. "What're you getting out of this, Turnbull?"

"Control of this place, on shares with Mrs. Banyan here."

Wanting time desperately, Derringer played for it as he never played out a weak, shaky hand of cards. While he could not understand how Calamity could have been arrested, he recalled that she had never come to the Big Herd. So the lawyer must be telling the truth. Nobody that Derringer knew of was aware of why he had left the wake—Rigg only found out by chance from a waiter who overheard the conversation in passing—so his disappearance would arouse no comment. Once the double killing had taken place, he did not doubt that a suitable story would be arranged. Yet Rigg was no fool. Given time, he might draw the right conclusions. All that remained was to stay alive long enough for that to happen.

"So you didn't tell him all of it, Counsellor," Derringer said.

"Shut your m——!" Gilbert barked.

"All?" interrupted Turnbull. "Is there something you left out, Lawyer?"

"Nothing!" Gilbert answered.

"Except about the Russians' jewellery that disappeared in the War," Derringer put in, watching anger darken Gilbert's features and interest flare in the saloon-keeper's eyes.

"Close your mouth, Der——!" Gilbert snarled, taking a Smith & Wesson revolver from under his coat.

"No, Derringer, you keep on talking!" Turnbull corrected. "Kill him if he tries to shoot, Ted."

"Easy enough done, even from here," Claggert answered, not moving from the bar.

Sitting on the edge of a nearby table, Derringer rested his cane against it. Clearly the men did not know of the cane's second purpose, for he had never advertised it. So he kept the weapon close to hand, ready for use if the chance arose. He could see that the mention of the Russians' jewellery had attracted both Rachel's and Turnbull's attention. Suspicion showed on their faces as they studied the lawyer.

"What's all this ab——" Rachel began, but the sound of two shots along the street chopped her words off. "That's Canary's finish, I should say."

Only by exerting all his willpower did Derringer prevent himself from grabbing the cane-gun. If Calamity had been killed, he wanted revenge but getting killed in a fruitless attempt would serve no useful purpose.

Then they heard the other shots and exchanged glances.

"She must have missed, or not killed Canary with the first shot," Rachel guessed, but the more experienced men noticed something that escaped her.

"There was a revolver as well as a carbine that time!" Turnbull stated.

"I told that fool Velma not to let Canary get a gun!" Rachel snapped. "But she either forgot, or couldn't prevent it. I hope Canary killed Sal. I can handle that man-hungry idiot Velma, but not Sal. Lord! You should have seen the way she killed Joan. With no more thought than I'd wash my face in a morning."

"Come on!" Gilbert put in. "Let's get it over with."

"Hoping they'll forget about the Russians' jewels, Counsellor?" Derringer asked, still fighting for time.

"Yeah, Lawyer," Turnbull said thoughtfully. "How about them?"

"What do I know about them?" snorted Gilbert, trying to sound convincing.

"You tried to have him killed for them," Derringer remarked.

"Me——!"

"It has to be you," Derringer insisted, raking his memory and coming up with answers. "Before he died, Sultan was rambling and he said something like 'There's no pretty gal at Tor Hill, Ed'——"

"That could mean Turnbull, even Claggert, or any of a dozen men in town!" the lawyer protested. "Anybody who knew Sultan'd know he'd go out to look over a pretty girl if he heard one was around."

"Sure," Derringer agreed. "But it wasn't Turnbull or Claggert. They'd want Sultan alive, so's they could fleece him with those marked cards."

"You tricky bastard, Derringer," Turnbull said admiringly. "You knew I was behind it all along."

"Not for sure. But it had to be somebody with contacts and money. You seemed the most likely. I was near enough sure when your man killed the dude to stop him talking. No, like I said, you was the only one, Counsellor. With Sultan dead, you, as his lawyer, could take over and run things——"

"But the will——?" Rachel began.

"He didn't know about the will until Doc Fir brought it to him," Derringer answered, still thinking back to the garbled, rambling utterances of the dying man. Fortunately for him, he had recently served as deputy under a mighty shrewd lawman and learned how to deduce from gathered, apparently meaningless, facts. So he could produce an answer to Gilbert's next objection.

"I've been with Sultan for years," the lawyer said. "Why should I suddenly decide to kill him?"

"Because time was running out. You'd hung around all those years just hoping to find the jewels. Then Sultan heard from somewhere that the Russians were dead. So he planned to take the jewels to Europe, sell them and have him a time. Folks still remembered the story in this country, so he daren't try to sell them over here. That's why you got him to Tor Hill and sent those hired guns after him. With him dead, you'd have the run of the saloon and could search every inch of it; which you'd never got the chance to do with him alive."

Nobody looking at Gilbert's shocked face could doubt that Derringer had called the play correctly. However, he rallied and gave a shrug, then said, "All right. So that's what I did. After all this time, with me sure the jewels are hid somewhere in the Harem, and he gets a letter from somebody back East telling him that those two Russians died in a yachting accident. Sultan never let on, but I knew what his vacation in Europe meant. He could sell the jewels over there. So I had to get rid of him——"

"And us, the wives?" Rachel hissed.

"So help me, I didn't know any of you existed!" spluttered the lawyer.

"Sultan sent for you to decide which one would go to Europe with him," Derringer went on. "And you all arrived the same day. Gilbert couldn't've known about you, or he'd've acted different."

"He'd still be running the place until you could be brought in," Turnbull remarked. "Time enough to search it."

"Is that why you've been so willing to help me?" Rachel asked Gilbert. "I thought there was something in it!"

"And you got me in on the game to take Derringer out of it, Lawyer," Turnbull growled. "Not that I blame you. He's smart and tough."

"The jewels are mine!" Rachel stated. "I am the only legal wife."

"You'll get some arguments about that," Derringer guessed.

"About the first part, they start right now," Turnbull went on. "It's a three-way split with them."

"Three!" Rachel squeaked.

"One, me. Two, the lawyer. Three, you. We're all in this together and none can do without the others. I need you and the lawyer to hold the saloon. You need me as protection against Sal's cowhands and the law. Three ways won't be so bad a split. Especially when all you figured getting was the saloon on half shares, Mrs. Banyan."

Anger flushed across Rachel's face, yet she knew that the saloon-keeper spoke the truth. From first learning of the other wives, she had schemed to gain full control of their husband's fortune. Not only did Banyan own the saloon but also he held interests in two of the mines, the hotel and other of the town's businesses. So she could afford to accept a third share of the jewels. Only an avaricious nature, and a certain snobbish objection to being ordered about by a man like Turnbull, caused her protests.

In avoiding meeting the men's eyes, Rachel looked around the room. She wanted time to think—and received something more to think about. Catching a movement with the corner of her eye, she turned her head and looked at the stairs. For one terrifying moment she thought the figure cautiously moving down was Sal. Then the truth burst on Rachel and she screamed her warning.

Dropping the whiskey bottle, Claggert thrust himself from the bar. He advanced in leaping strides, swinging toward the direction at which Rachel pointed. Up on the stairs, Calamity saw the man emerge. Remembering the callous way that the floor-boss had killed Woodley, she did not hesitate. Whipping up her arm, she hurled the grenade. In the poor light and at that distance she could only hope to hit the man. The hope did not materialize, although Calamity had no call to complain about the result of the miss; it might almost be said that missing proved more effective.

Down plunged the grenade, its stabilizing fins keeping the head pointing in the correct position. Missing Claggert, the base flange made contact with the floor between him and the bar. The impact caused the percussion cap to collide with the head of the plunger. With a roar, the grenade exploded. Caught in the blast, Claggert gave one hideous scream before his torn-open body went to the floor. In addition to killing the man, the force of the explosion ripped a hole in the floorboards.

Taken by surprise even though Claggert's body had shielded them from the main force of the explosion, the others on the floor froze for a moment. First to recover, Derringer caught up and raised the cane. Just as Turnbull started to line his revolver, Derringer pressed the cane's firing stud. Flame followed the cork plug and bullet from the ferrule. Angling upward, the .38 bullet drove into Turnbull's head. Twisting around on the impact, nervous reaction of the muscles sent the saloon-keeper's body staggering away. The Colt dropped from his fingers, then his body crumpled and crashed to the floor.

With Turnbull taken out of the fight, Derringer swung his attention to the lawyer. Thrusting himself from the table. Derringer swung his cane. He missed death by inches as the light-caliber Smith & Wesson spat and sent its bullet by his head. Lashing around, the heavy barrel of the cane crashed into the lawyer's shoulder; the left one unfortunately. Even as Derringer's injured leg buckled under him, he saw Calamity leaping down the stairs and Gilbert reeling away from him. Stumbling across the room, the lawyer came to a halt almost on the edge of the hole in the floor. He snarled with rage and began to raise his revolver for a careful aim.

Although down in a semi-kneeling position, Derringer did not hesitate. He hurled the cane in a spinning flight across the room. Seeing it flying toward his head, Gilbert threw up an arm to ward it off and took an involuntary pace to the rear. Just too late he realized his danger. The rearmost foot met empty air. With a scream the lawyer tumbled backward and disappeared down the hole. Although neither Derringer nor Calamity noticed it, the sound of Gilbert's arrival at the bottom came as a splash, not a thud.

Face twisted in rage, Rachel darted to where Turnbull's revolver lay and she bent to pick it up. By that time Calamity had reached the foot of the stairs and started toward the woman. Tossing the Navy Colt in a border shift from the right to left hand, Calamity freed and swung her whip. Like a flash the lash hissed through the air, its popper tip snapping savagely against Rachel's rump. Unlike Velma, Rachel did not wear a bustle. So only three thin layers of cloth covered her flesh. The hardened leather tip sliced through dress, underskirt and drawers like a knife into butter. Fingers already closed on and lifting the Colt, Rachel felt the searing, unexpected pain. A screech broke from her lips, she jerked erect but the revolver remained clutched in her hand.

Twisting around, Rachel brought up the gun with both hands. Calamity did not hesitate. Back, around and out circled the whip's lash. True as one could desire, it curled forward, driving below the raised arms to bite into Rachel's body. A scream burst from the woman and Derringer saw bare flesh beneath the clothing torn by the whip. Letting the Colt drop, Rachel clutched at her side with both hands. Back swung the whip, carrying its lash in the rearward part of another attack. Sobbing, Rachel stumbled against a table but Calamity prepared to strike again.

"No, Calam!" Derringer yelled. "Don't!"

Shock as much as anything caused Calamity to lower her whip. She stared in amazement at the blood running through the tear in Rachel's bodice and realized that the lash had caused it. While knowing her whip to be a deadly weapon, Calamity realized for the first time its full potential.

The side door burst open. Coming through, gun in hand, Like-His Rigg skidded to a halt and glared around the room as if hardly able to believe his eyes.

"What in hell——?" he started.

"It's all over," Derringer replied, hauling himself erect. "If Doc Fir's around, you'd best get him in here."

After collecting the doctor and ordering the rest of the assembled people to stay back, Rigg closed the saloon's door. He took possession of Turnbull's Colt, watch Fir approach and examine Rachel, then looked around. Giving a wry grunt, he passed over the gory remains of Claggert, took in Turnbull's body and then swung to face Derringer.

"Where's Gilbert?"

"He fell into the cellar there," the gambler replied.

Taking the bull's eye lantern from the table, Rigg crossed to the hole. Calamity followed him and they looked downward. However, the light of the lantern did not show the cellar. Instead it illuminated a round shaft sunk into the rock and faintly down below water glinted. For a moment the implications of what they saw did not strike them. Then Calamity straightened up and looked at the deputy. There seemed to be only one comment to make.

"Well, well, well!" she said.

Chapter 17

WHILE THE DOCTOR ATTENDED TO RACHEL'S BLEED-ing side and diagnosed a broken rib, Derringer told Rigg everything he knew. The deputy listened in silence, then stated he considered the gambler had acted correctly throughout; even to not mentioning Banyan's dying words about the treasure in the well. However, Rigg continued, they must wait to hear what his uncle said on the matter. Sufficient evidence remained for him to hold Rachel in jail until the sheriff returned, so he left Derringer and went to attend to her incarceration.

By the time the sheriff returned at noon, Rigg had placed Calamity before the witness from the hotel. The woman stated that Calamity had not been the person seen fleeing from the murder room. That cleared Calamity, but Rachel steadfastly refused to make any comment. In addition to proving Calamity innocent, Rigg allowed himself to be lowered on a rope down the well shaft. He found the Russians' jewellery box in a niche carved into the rock above the water level and brought it to the surface. Retrieving Gilbert's body did not prove so easy.

On his return, Sheriff Wendley heard the full story of the events in town. Then he explained how he and Turk had trailed Nabbes. There had been shooting, in which Nabbes and Turk both died. However, Ferrely—who had been left with the horses while the others stalked the camp—convinced the sheriff that Derringer had told the truth. After burying Turk, Wendley made for Tor Hill. There he learned that only one Banyan resident had visited the village in the past couple of weeks: Gilbert. Heading back to town with the intention of questioning the lawyer, he arrived to find everything settled—or almost everything.

The rightful ownership of the jewellery would need to be decided. Also a case against Rachel made and put through the courts. Still maintaining her silence, she gave no hint that might help convict her as an accessory to murder. Like-His Rigg headed for the Territorial capital as fast as a horse could carry him, under orders to ask the Governor's attorney for advice.

Between them, from information gathered and guesswork, Derringer and Wendley constructed the whole story. Without his men knowing it, Sultan Banyan must have brought the Russians' property from the Bushwhacker camp and hidden it. Later, maybe even after the War's end, he collected the loot. The money gave him his start out west, but the jewellery could not be sold as long as its owners lived. Chinese coolies built the Harem, constructing the well in secret, and returned to San Francisco on its completion. With his loot safely hidden, Banyan waited for its owners to die. He had sufficient confidence to take the trips on which he married the three other wives. Subsequent investigations showed that his various business interests had kept all four women in comfort. Although unable to locate the jewellery, Gilbert knew of the business interests. So he could satisfy Rachel's curiosity when she asked about them. Probably each of them realized that the other would be useful and they formed an alliance; with Gilbert hoping to achieve his ends and Rachel planning how to gain control of her late husband's entire estate.

A week went by and Like-His Rigg returned with orders to hold the jewellery pending the arrival of the attorney. Much discussion had taken place on the matter of Rachel, the deputy reported, with the result that she would be tried only for her part in attempting to murder Derringer. Even that would be no straightforward case as Calamity learned when the sheriff sent for her.

"He allows that we should say nothing about me being at the saloon," she told the gathering of people in the Harem's private office. "I didn't hear anything they said and can only tie things in knots."

"How about the killings at the jail?" Derringer inquired.

"Way they'll tell it, Sal killed Velma over the will, or out of meanness, and got shot by the deputy. It's the only hope they've got of nailing Rachel's hide to the wall—— And maybe the sheriff reckons it'll be safer with me out of town."

"He could be right," Derringer said, eyeing the girl. "You're likely to do something loco if you stay on."

"Thing being, my share in the saloon here," Calamity said, turning her eyes to Goldie and the other senior employees. "You all know that I don't reckon I've any claim to it——"

"That's not what the boss said," Sharp put in.

"You won't let me give it to you, my share, I mean?"

"No!" the reply came from all the employees. Then Sharp went on, "Derry's staying, why not you?"

"Like I said, I don't have any claim——!" Calamity began.

"You've as much as me," Derringer commented. "Sultan was a gambler and left things that way on purpose."

"All right, I'm a gambler as well," Calamity answered. "You folks willing to gamble with me? One cut of the cards. If you win, I stay. If I win, you bunch take my share."

"That's fair enough to me," Derringer commented, knowing that the girl intended to leave and wanting to help her. Before any of the others could accept or refuse, he took a deck of cards from the desk drawer and shuffled them thoroughly. Placing them before the girl, he said, "Yours, Calam."

"You first, Goldie," Calamity objected. "You gents don't mind us girls settling this, now do you?"

None of the men objected, for the sporting nature of the affair would satisfy their dead boss's sense of the fitness of things. So Goldie cut about a quarter of the way down the deck. Guessing that Calamity wanted to lose, the blonde hoped for a high card.

"Four of spades," she said a touch bitterly, exposing her choice.

Calamity cut, glanced at the card and replaced the portion she held on to the top of the deck without allowing anybody to see it.

"My! Aren't I the unlucky one," she said. "Deuce."

"*Deuce?*" repeated Goldie before she could stop herself.

Picking up the cards, Calamity began to sort through them. To Derringer at least it was obvious that she had passed the place at which she cut her card. Then, with a slight sigh of relief, she tossed the deuce of hearts before the others.

"Like I said," she announced, trying to look like a disappointed loser. "A deuce!"

"As fine a one as there ever was," Derringer agreed. "You've just lost half a saloon, Calamity gal."

"It sure looks that way," she replied, and the old, reckless Calamity grin creased her face. "Damn! I allus knowed that gambling'd be the ruin of me."